D1526235

THE DOLLAR
COVENANT

MICHAEL SINCLAIR

THE DOLLAR COVENANT

W·W· NORTON & COMPANY · INC·

NEW YORK

Library of Congress Cataloging in Publication Data
Sinclair, Michael.
The dollar covenant.
    I. Title.
PZ4.S6158Do3 [PR6069.I54]   823'.9'14   73-8926
ISBN 0-393-08369-1
PRINTED IN THE UNITED STATES OF AMERICA

        1 2 3 4 5 6 7 8 9 0

To M.D.D.S. and I.S.

For convenience, the events in this book can be thought of as taking place some few years hence. But this is in no way a futuristic book and the action could, in different circumstances, be taking place now.

THE DOLLAR
COVENANT

I WAS STILL far from expert. The wheels had a will of their own which I had yet to master even when my strength allowed. Despite the bitterness of the sea wind, I was pouring with sweat by the time I was half way to the roadside.

Ingram, an unenthusiastic spectator of my sudden lust for exercise and fresh air, left the Rover and came up behind me. But he had a sullen percipience, Ingram, and, sensing my mood, he withheld his offer of help. I would get there on my own.

Behind me, the sand, the rocks and an advancing tide. A sand-castle, built with the expertise of some local child more practised than any young visitor from the City, was, despite walls well armoured with limpet shells and pebbles against the sea, gradually being eroded as the waves circled it.

I forced the wheelchair to the road up an incline that a two-year-old could, unaided, have wandered up in a moment, yet, at the summit, I sat resting in satisfaction at my achievement. I turned the big wheels counter to each other and faced the sea again. The landside wall of the sand-castle sank gently into an anonymous pile of wet sludge as I watched, and only the centre keep remained unharmed. The water was nearly at the higher line of seaweed and the fate of the structure now depended on whether the tide turned soon, and the January wind dropped.

Ingram returned to the car, impatiently slapping his hands together against the cold. Let him wait. The air might bring a touch of colour to that pale, unhealthy face, might dilute the odour of stale cigarette smoke that perpetually hung around him. An odd man Ingram, but I think he respected me and he certainly valued his job.

I sat there, braced more than numbed by the wind. I had on a short sheepskin coat; only my legs, in thin camouflaging pin-stripes, would be cold if I could have felt them. A touch of refrigeration could add nothing to what had already been done.

Over to the right, the road ran down and along by the shore. The bungalows hadn't been allowed to scatter as far as this and a large wooded estate still occupied the landward side, its trees permanently, grotesquely bent by the prevailing on-shore wind. Beyond, and sheltered by the wood, lay the neat black fields of rich Berwickshire soil. In this part of the country, life had gone on as prosperously as before; some had even gained from independence, unlike those I knew and understood better, who lived in the grey industrial belt to the north-west.

Sitting there, the cold sea ahead, I felt detached, as if I were uninvolved, as if I could do nothing to alleviate the problems that tore at the unity of the country. Yet the story was only half way told. The beginning had already been, and my escape could last no more than a few moments, even if my despatch box had not been there on the back seat of the Rover, as a constant reminder. A lid embossed with gilt symbolic thistle and the title of my office, and under it, the buff files that contained the problems. Neatly and coldly, my officials had digested and presented them; but on their stiff blue-crested paper, they were, by and large, mine to solve.

And these were my public problems. There were others, some of which the public knew about—like my injury, my wheelchair; some they did not, like my private wreck of a life and marriage. The public, most of my colleagues, granted me too much sympathy, too much consideration for the former; but even my few close friends gave little for the latter. The reason was simple. They did not know. Only my doctors knew a part, and Angela. Angela is my wife.

The flakes of sleet must have been hitting me for some moments because my coat was quite white when Ingram screwed up courage and shiveringly disturbed me.

"Are you all right, Minister?" His voice was anxious more about my reaction than about me, since my temper, always uneven, had hardly benefited from my injury. But Ingram shouldn't have worried. I would manage to control it with him.

He was, after all, not only my driver but my legs as well.

"Of course. You're cold?" My voice was still a fraction too sharp. "Very well then. Let's get me back inside. I have that meeting at three."

I wheeled myself across the road to the near-side rear door of the Rover, and the elaborate procedure of loading me and my chair into the back began all over again. But, between us, we were getting better at it, and the Ministry garage had done an efficient job of moving one of the seats to allow more space for the manœuvre.

Inside the car, I had just taken the silver top from my hip-flask when the radio-telephone began to bleep.

ONE

A RHYTHMIC SPIRAL of water pouring from a fractured gutter close under the grey slates. It made little impression on a century and a half of engrained grime as it hit the projecting lintel above a doorway. Most of the water drained away in rivulets down to the pavement flagstones, but enough was retained to provide nourishment for the bright green crops of moss that flourished along the crevices where dirty red sandstone fitted unevenly against rotting door-frames.

The heavy grey of the clouds, only a fraction lighter in tone than the surrounding buildings, was aided by the teeming rain in blurring into uncertainty the line where the street's roof-tops met the sky. Every surface slimy and decaying to the touch, and the rain, rather than cleaning and refreshing as it fell, becoming immediately infected by the misery of its new environment. Running among the cobblestones to the blocked drains by the kerbside, it joined the polluted pools, gradually stretching out from each side to meet and form a barricade across the street.

The water, the rain and the high damp walls of the squalid tenements provided an all too effective trap for the small band of marchers. A wet Monday morning, it was also the fourth anniversary of Independence, and Clydebank's Republican contingent was making its sodden way through the deserted backstreets to meet up with the main procession for the big rally in St George's Square.

Police Constable Wraight, brought in from his quiet rural beat at Lennoxtown, to help a hard-pressed City Constabulary for the day, was one of the regulation handful of police escorts. He submitted his report later. The policemen's style was terse and unpolished.

The number of party faithfuls was much down in size compared with attendance figures for previous years. The

organisers comforted themselves by telling each other that the
rain had kept people at home, but they knew the ten per cent
unemployment and the big strike meant that few had feeling or
energy left for celebration this Monday morning.

The crowd was big enough to get itself into disorder, not
helped by the participants having to ford the flooded street.
The three pipers at the head neither faltered nor lost step, but
those who came after were less resolute and the whole procession came to a halt while discipline was reintroduced to the
ranks. The police escort took advantage of the hold-up to take
a moment or two's shelter in a doorway. PC Wraight, no
Scotsman judging by his name, cursed the weather, the dirt of
the City and the stridency of the pipe music with equal vigour.

The respite was brief; the procession, hesitantly, moved
forward once again. Pulling the collars of their capes up
around their necks, the policemen returned to their positions
and to the rain.

By the gates of the idle, deserted shipyard, the marchers
turned a corner into another anonymous, dirty street lined with
boarded-up shops. For a moment the rain and the misery
obscured the view. Then the leaders saw the men waiting for
them. A crowd of some three hundred of the strikers, spread
right across the street ahead, standing silent, black and yellow
industrial helmets glistening in the morning rain.

The Police Sergeant in charge shouted an order. PC Wraight
spoke urgently into his transistorised radio. Back at Constabulary Headquarters an alarm bell sounded.

By now only fifty yards separated the two groups, the
Republicans outnumbered at least four to one. The shipyard
strikers weren't there by accident, and wouldn't clear a path
without trouble. Both sides knew their enemy. It had happened
too often before.

"Keep going," shouted the procession leader. "Keep going.
We've a right to go through and the police here will see we're
all right." The man's look belied the confidence of his words.
Half a dozen policemen wouldn't go far.

Down to ten yards and the procession hesitated and slowed down. The three pipers continued to blow resolutely but marked time awaiting further instructions.

PC Wraight and two of his colleagues moved ahead in an attempt to clear a way through the motionless, eerily silent wall of men. Tension had reached breaking-point. The only sound came from the pipes. High up, a few anxious female heads watched from top storey tenement windows.

"Move along there. This is an authorised procession." PC Wraight confidently addressed the front rank strikers. No one moved at first, then surprisingly, with some shuffling, a narrow but orderly path was cleared ahead. PC Wraight muttered some hopeful words of commentary into his two-way radio. At Headquarters the alarm bell continued to ring.

The procession advanced deep into the crowd, pushing its way along the reluctant path between the silent men. The three policemen were a few steps ahead, and the pipers were keeping manfully in tune. Even the rain seemed to be easing a little.

When the procession was about half way through, PC Wraight heard, coming from his left, a shrill, deliberate whistle cut above the sound of the pipes. At once the strikers closed in; the music died instantly. A set of bagpipes flew incongruously through the air. Wraight seized his radio, but strong hands grabbed him from behind, a sack was thrown over his head, and he felt himself carried like a child through a mass of surging bodies. There were muffled sounds of shouting, a scream of intense male agony close at hand, then the clattering of steel-capped boots on the cobblestones.

A few moments and Wraight knew he was away from the main crowd, but with his arms and legs expertly locked by several pairs of hands, he was unable to resist. He felt one of his captors stumble, a door slammed somewhere beside him, and the sound of shouting in the background became fainter.

"We've no great quarrel wi' the polis," a deep voice muttered through the sack in his ear. "But any funny business and ye'll get the same as they Republican scum." Thrown roughly on to a floor Wraight felt his hands being tied behind him. Further muttering followed, though not addressed to him, and then there was silence.

He sensed he was alone. Gently he tested the ropes. He had been hurriedly and unskilfully tied, and he easily worked himself free. Cautiously he reached up and removed the sack from his head.

The little bare room was empty and almost in darkness, though a little light filtered in from a skylight above the door. At a guess he was in what had been a coal cellar. He felt for his two-way radio but it was gone. He stood up shakily, and as he did so his foot scraped against something metallic. The broken remnants of the radio lay beside him on the dirty stone floor. He left it and moved over to the door. Jammed rather than locked, it gave easily when he ran at it with his shoulder. He went through into what was the close of one of the tenements, and from there into the street.

Blinking in the dull light, he arrived back on the scene at precisely the same moment as the police squad cars. The sodden street was littered with bodies and broken banners. Not a striker was to be seen. Wraight stumbled over towards his colleagues as they emerged from their shiny black cars. On his way he accidentally trod on a set of abandoned bagpipes which let out a last low moan of sound. At last the rain had stopped.

TWO

THE COMMISSIONER OF POLICE took his tea without milk or sugar. I remembered that in his own office he had it served in a glass, tea leaves carefully excluded by a little silver strainer, so that it took on the appearance of a pale malt whisky. It was an affectation in peculiar contrast with his robust military approach and apparent lack of any subtlety. The rest of us were served with rather nasty instant coffee, so perhaps the Commissioner had a point.

I had arrived back in the City centre just in time for the meeting; an informal gathering in my room. Mine was an agreeable office on the third floor of the new National Assembly building, with a bright, open outlook down to Princes Street and what the City Council had left of the New Town. My Permanent Secretary, the Under-Secretary in charge of the Division and the Secretary to the Cabinet were already there talking to the Commissioner. Guthrie, my Private Secretary, hovered in the background ready to take the confidential record. They all stood up as I wheeled myself across to my desk. I could see from the grave looks on their faces that they too had heard about the riot.

"What's the score?" I asked impassively.

"Five dead, and at least twenty seriously injured, Minister," said my Permanent Secretary.

We were all quiet for a moment. It was the worst yet. Then I turned abruptly and irritably to the matter in hand; "Police morale, Gentlemen. That's the agenda. Other things can wait." Sometimes, like now, I had a glimpse of why many thought I was heartless. These busy, intelligent men all wanted to go on talking, gossiping about the riot. I saw little point. It had happened; we knew why; that was the end of it.

The Commissioner opened the discussion straightaway,

without being asked. It was typically direct of him, and though I had wanted to set the tone of the meeting, introducing my own ideas from the outset, I let him go on. It was a considerable mistake.

He was brashly confident, or appeared so. The police were ninety-nine per cent loyal to authority, and the only problem, in his view, was the political one of ensuring that the authority did not change. That was my problem, he told me impertinently. The one per cent were unreliable solely because in some Section Houses and in one or two Districts, pressures and tensions in the surrounding communities had proved too strong. But the Commissioner had that well in hand. He had already appointed a special Personnel Review Committee within his central policy department to review cases and cross-post drastically. Two Constabulary Sub-Districts had already been entirely broken up and re-staffed.

The Police Commissioner sat back in the heavy, brown leather arm-chair, and sipped at his cup. To me, and, I would guess, to the others, he appeared complacent rather than confident. I had seen the Special Branch reports which suggested very much less contentment in the Section Houses. Should I burst his bubble?

MacDowall did it for me. Leaning forward he pursed his lips into what might have been intended as a smile. His rimless half-moon glasses, at once fashionable and unfashionable, were perched exactly in the middle of a long drooping nose. They were glasses to be looked over rather than through, and they symbolised the man. Tall, stooping, Sir Alexander MacDowall, Secretary to the Cabinet, the sole tenant of that office since independence, was a man who, in my less optimistic moods of trust in the democratic process, I sometimes felt ran the country more than any of us. MacDowall the awe-inspiring old régimer of Scottish Office days, who had held on to office after the change because it was his by right and no one felt able or sure enough to take it away from him; the man of whom the Prime Minister, in an unguarded, indiscreet and exceptionally perspicacious moment, had said that underneath that cold exterior there beat a heart of ice. I liked and tried to emulate this coldness, but outwardly I failed because of my too-ready temper, just as inwardly, I hoped, I still had some warmth left somewhere.

"I feel we might be straying into making dangerous assumptions by extrapolating present content into an uneasy future," he began remotely. I knew the tone and foresaw that the Police Commissioner would take offence later when he realised the veiled criticisms behind the pedantic, carefully chosen words. But not yet. MacDowall was still being both diplomatic and obscure.

"It may be," he went on, "that the five—I'm sorry . . . did you say one per cent—discontent in the Police Force could be successfully dissipated were the political climate a static one. But we are in a rapidly developing situation and I would not be honest if I did not say that I think we are in for a period of worsening tensions. We probably agree on that?" He looked round enquiringly as he always did in Cabinet, and seldom did he reap a dissident voice.

He did this time. "I'm only a simple policeman," began the Police Commissioner. I watched MacDowall's lips mouthing; "Quite so." No one else noticed.

"I may only be a policeman, but I feel that there is too much pessimism in some quarters. I have the utmost faith in the good sense and discipline of the Force."

"I fully subscribe to that latter sentiment," MacDowall retorted, "if, if present conditions prevail."

I stepped in, since I saw that the Police Commissioner was beginning to bridle. It would not do to have a clash at this early stage. The trouble was, MacDowall was too used to running if not bullying the Cabinet. He ought to have shown more tact.

"We all have the utmost faith in the Force," I said. "But in the worst event, a general breakdown of law and order, could you cope? There's precious little of an army left to back you up, and calling out the Volunteer Reserve would be foolish in these circumstances, as you all know." The Volunteer Reservists were loyalist to a man and would simply exacerbate the situation.

"That's your problem, Minister," replied the Police Commissioner smugly. "Discipline will go elsewhere—in the Civil Service for example—before it goes with us." He glared with hostility at my officials as he spoke. "We can cope—especially if you arm us."

"You know that's impossible." I was short. My resolve to keep the peace between him and MacDowall evaporated with my growing anger.

The Commissioner looked at me coldly, and then, as if deliberately trying to provoke me, he went on: "At the moment, maybe, Minister. But if we had been armed this past year, lots of things might have been very, very different." He paused. "Take today's riot in Glasgow. Five is a lot of dead."

He was making a direct reference to my long-standing opposition to giving the police weapons; indirectly he was suggesting I myself was responsible for the attack which had put me in a wheelchair. Everyone looked at me. I flushed and started to erupt. As I wheeled myself round to face the Commissioner, I felt it coming but was equally powerless to check it. Guthrie also saw it coming. He moved his chair abruptly forward and upset the coffee table as if by accident. In the general confusion and apologising I subsided once again. But from then on the meeting was a dead loss. Each of us said our piece but at the end nothing was agreed except that we should keep in touch. We should have to do that in any case.

When they had all left, Guthrie brought in a messenger with a bucket and cloth to try to get the coffee stains out of the carpet.

"I suppose I should be grateful to you," I muttered. Guthrie pretended not to have heard.

A wasted hour later, I left. A uniformed usher saluted with

regimental precision, but as the floor of the main foyer was on a slight slope, I couldn't take my hands from the wheels to acknowledge it. I nodded my acceptance instead. As my chair ran over the tripboards, the huge plate-glass doors opened automatically and I rolled myself out into the grey Edinburgh afternoon.

Over by the main gates of the National Assembly building, a newsvendor's placards carried the latest unemployment figures, the highest since the 'thirties, so they proclaimed. To hell. We had had it all out at Friday's Cabinet Meeting and my cautious suggestion that they be witheld for *technical reasons* until after the debate had met with little response. The Secretary to the Cabinet had whispered a shocked defence of democratic practice into the PM's ear and that was an end of it. I have no need to defend my record on matters of democracy, but there are occasions such as this where the *national interest* clause in the Constitution could well be utilised. I warned them of the consequences and it went into the Cabinet Minutes for posterity to judge.

My official Rover glided across the forecourt, and stopped beside me. Ingram climbed out, uneasily adjusting his shoulder holster as he did so. I had protested a little when Special Branch recommended that he be armed after the attack on me, but while I was convalescing, they had put him through a three-weeks' small-arms course at Rosyth. Ingram himself was pleased with the extra status it gave him. It also impressed his wife.

He came round to help me with my chair and gave me the news with a grin. I presume he thought it would please or satisfy me to hear that MacManus's appeal had been rejected by the High Court, that the twelve-year sentence on the man who had killed me from the waist down still stood.

"He'll no starve in Peterhead Jail," Ingram said happily. I was numb to the remark and to the memory that MacManus had six children and had been out of work for as many months. The law had taken its course, whatever I thought. No one had asked me how many years in jail my paralysis was worth. Presumably judges and jury had weighed it carefully on the traditional scales of justice. Two legs: twelve years: six apiece. Had I been on the bench instead, I might have been understanding, tolerant, put him on probation for the sake of his six children. But as I am Minister of Home Affairs, and half a physical man to boot, an example had to be made, and long years behind the granite walls of Peterhead are not only just, but also necessary, for the sake of national law and order.

So, at the news, I showed none of the emotion for which Ingram had been waiting. In consequence he looked a little despondent. It was not that he was a malicious man, but he was of the Free Church, and a believer in the wrath of God. Fortunately the courts could not pass a sentence of paralysis.

"We're late for the opening," I said abruptly, manœuvring myself into the back seat. It was a long-standing commitment to inaugurate the new Operations Room for the Glasgow CID and, in the aftermath of the riot, there would be a lot of press interest in my attendance. As Ingram slammed the door behind me I made a mental note to find out how MacManus's family were getting on. A little charity might not come amiss.

We drove down The Mound to Princes Street and turned left along towards Haymarket to pick up the approach road to the Glasgow Motorway. Pulling my body upright, I moved my legs into a more comfortable position on the black leather seat, and settled back for the hour's drive. The sun had gone again and some sudden flecks of rain spattered the windscreen.

I thought back to Saturday morning's interview with William Torrance, the official representative in Edinburgh of the Federation of American Caledonian Societies. After the initial pleasantries, after Torrance had hesitantly asked if we could speak privately and Guthrie had withdrawn to his office, the message had been blunt enough. It had been sensible too, in its way. But it needed thinking about and I had played for time. My totally non-committal attitude had worried Torrance; I could have drafted his anxious report to his Chairman, Mac-

Pake in New York. But he needn't worry. The proposal was safe. In its way it was flattering that it had been I whom the Americans had chosen to approach. I appreciated the Federation's anxiety and shared it.

But how to play it? How could I conceivably be the funnel for millions of dollars of aid without everyone knowing, and Ian Campbell, Governor of the Reserve Bank, first of all? It was an absurdly impossible task. In duty bound I should have reported it straightaway to the Prime Minister, got it off my chest. I had enough to worry about. But I had hesitated. I hadn't gone to the PM. The PM was past it, an elderly relic of the Great Struggle rather than the *eminence grise* of his popular public image. If that were so, were there not some of my other colleagues in Cabinet who could help? They weren't all like Dr McKinnon. He was too much the extremist who would curse the offer and the promises that went with it. In any case I didn't like the man and McKinnon didn't like me. It wouldn't work. What of some of the others? Matthews of the Department of Trade, for example? A stickler for legality and correct procedures, he would insist on informing the PM and Cabinet. Then I had thought about the man who, more than anyone, had a grip of what was going on—MacDowall, the Secretary to the Cabinet.

My thoughts were interrupted by the sight of a man gesticulating outside the car window. We had stopped briefly at the last set of traffic lights before hitting the Motorway. An old man was standing beside the car in a greasy gaberdine and an old tweed cap, his face contorted with dislike. He had recognised me—I am not one of those politicians who doesn't look the part—and whatever his reasons, his feelings were obviously intense. He started hammering at the window in his anger. "Twelve years," I heard him shout. "Twelve years of a man's life." Ingram turned sharply in his seat, his hand moving up automatically to his shoulder holster.

The incident was short-lived. A policeman appeared from nowhere, and also recognising me, pulled the old man away.

The lights changed and we left them. I managed to heave myself round and look out of the back window at the little group that had gathered beside the traffic lights. The old man was still waving wildly in my direction.

I had grown immune to most political insults, since the majority of them were surface affairs and personal relationships seldom suffered underneath. In any case I gave as good as I got and it was part of the fabric of all political life. It was the same with public abuse; every politician has to face up to demonstrations and heckling, but it too is generally of an impersonal kind. It was the other things that had hurt me, the individual personalised attacks, on television, in the newspapers and elsewhere, the conventional, generally accepted wisdom that in some way I, as Minister of Home Affairs, had been personally responsible for many of the misfortunes of the country. That had hurt. It had been unjust and untrue, as those in the know realised. But that hadn't helped. I had rapidly become identified as the public enemy, the focus of every discontent.

Then came the attack on me by MacManus, an unemployed ship-yard worker. It had two results: it had put me in hospital for months, leaving me a paralysed wreck, and it had stilled the critics' voices overnight. The fickle public, led by the press, had shed a guilty tear and I was suddenly overwhelmed with sympathy and regrets. Now when they spoke of me, they set my actions in a totally uncritical light, they prefaced every editorial with sickening references to my disability and my supposed courage in keeping at my Ministry desk. I became the martyr, the man who had fought and fallen, injured for his principles, principles which had suddenly become respectable. Others had taken on the role of public bogeymen.

Perhaps the old man at the traffic lights hadn't heard about my martydom, that the pack were hunting on a different trail. Perhaps he knew MacManus or his family; perhaps he was just more honest than the rest and believed that my principles and policies couldn't have changed so rapidly. Whatever his reasons, to me it was an unpleasant reminder of the past and of the timely benefit, at least in political terms, of my physical state.

In present circumstances, however, conditions prevailed in which I could do nothing wrong. Almost nothing. But even I could scarcely carry off this American financing scheme without help. So I had bought time. I had asked Torrance to provide me with more details: how much money would be forthcoming; what time-scale he foresaw; and most important, what were the strings? Generous as the Federation had been in the past, I could not believe that there would be no conditions attached to a rescue operation of this scale; Torrance had done nothing to deny that these would be forthcoming.

In the meantime, I would do nothing except discuss the offer with the Secretary to the Cabinet. I had been non-committal, and had told Torrance I would need a lot of persuading, that Scotland had a long way to go before it need become a beggar.

Torrance had looked wise; I knew that he appreciated the reasons for my expression of false optimism.

I pushed the little button which operated the electric blinds covering the Rover's side windows, eased myself into a slightly less uncomfortable position on the seat and prepared to sleep. I needed every minute.

THREE

THE SKYLIGHT WAS unfastened as he had been promised it would be. The man in the gloves produced a small oil can and gently applied it along both of the protruding hinges, waited a few moments till it penetrated the slight rust, and then, inserting his fingers under the rim, raised the skylight carefully. There was hardly a sound. He rested the heavy frame back against a concrete chimney stack.

He climbed across, suspended himself lightly over the hole, then lowered himself carefully into the darkness. There should be a table, down and slightly to the left, which he would just be able to reach with his feet. For an instant he swung precariously in space till his feet found the promised foothold, then finding his balance, he let go with his hands and softly eased himself from the table to the ground.

A pencil torch produced from his inside pocket shed a thin beam of light round the little room. The walls were lined with old newspapers neatly arranged on steel racks. The glass door was open and a chipped sign stencilled on the nameplate read *Presscuttings Section*. There was a musty dust-laden smell in the air.

Through he went to the linoleum-covered landing, then down two flights. He remembered to step over the second top step of the lower flight because it creaked badly. It wasn't meant to matter since the building should be entirely empty. He must be on the correct floor now. Deep brown carpeting had replaced the noisy linoleum and the walls were hung with rather stark modern American paintings. The large double-door facing him must be the one. He went up to it, examining it carefully, confirming this to himself. He bent down.

He placed his torch on the floor so that it shone at the wall, and produced a small screwdriver. Holding it in his gloved hands, he eased away a little square of skirting board which fitted, almost unnoticeable, at the bottom of the doorframe. It came away easily. Behind it, screwed to the wall, was the junction box for the burglar alarm system. He noted the disconnected wire that had allowed him to pass through the skylight unannounced. He took his screwdriver and disconnected one of the other screws carefully. Marked with a red blob of paint, this one fed the circuit round the double-door and also covered the safe in the room itself. Whoever had defused the skylight had not been able to neutralise this one, since it alone was always checked by the guard last thing at night. For the tenth time that night the man in the gloves hoped that the Special Task Unit had prepared the ground well.

Having double-checked his instructions, he straightened up and faced the door. The key was on a string round his waist. The ring end was oddly shaped, the business end should be exactly right. It was a moulded copy of the original, after all. The wax in a cigarette box trick had seen to that, so they had told him. He took the oil can out again, and applied a few drops to the key. Inserting it gently into the lock, he turned it easily. There was no sound and he reached for the handle.

For a moment he thought something had gone wrong, that there must be another lock. But he had misjudged the weight of the oak door, which opened ponderously at the second attempt.

Despite the modern furniture it was an elegant room, dominated by the rosewood desk in the centre. Steel and black leather armchairs were scattered around a low marble-topped coffee table by the Adam fireplace. In the corner, the only thing decidedly out of keeping in the room was the safe, a squat, ugly steel box, bolted to the floor. The dials of the two combination locks were set into the door.

The man took his gloves off. Setting the correct combination would require a light touch, and he had a wet cloth in his pocket to remove any finger-prints afterwards. Holding the pencil torch in his mouth, he took a piece of paper from his hip pocket and re-read the numbers on it. He started turning the top dial slowly, alternately clockwise and anti-clockwise. He dialled a different set of numbers on the bottom dial, pulled the lever handles and the safe door opened. If all safe-breaking jobs were as easy as this he would now be a rich man, and not just out on promised permanent parole from Peterhead Jail.

File number XK 1739 was a red folder on the top shelf. *Top Secret* labels were stuck diagonally across the front. The title read *Correspondence with the President of the Federation*, just as they had said.

The man moved across to the desk and placed the file on it. He opened up his jacket and from a small plastic bag suspended round his neck, took out a miniature camera with flash gun attachment. He adjusted it briefly, still holding the torch in his mouth. Then extinguishing the light for a moment, he went across to the windows to ensure that the curtains were properly drawn. Back to the desk, he began to photograph the contents of the file, each page of each letter, turning them carefully by the very tip of the page to leave no prints. He didn't bother to read what they said. That wasn't his business nor part of the contract with the men who had come to his cell yesterday and who had so startlingly promised him freedom in return for his professional services.

Half an hour and two changes of film later, he had finished. He wiped the file carefully, and returned it to its precise position in the safe. And as he did so, he noticed the small cash box on one of the lower shelves. With an effort he ignored it, not out of any scruple, but because he knew his contacts would be waiting outside for him to account for his visit.

He shut the safe and twirled the dials till they locked, then, carefully and deliberately, retraced his steps, checking each action as he completed it. He wiped the safe, left the room, relocked the door with the odd-shaped key, re-set the burglar alarm, replaced the section of skirting board, and climbed the stairs to the top floor once again.

The last stage was the most difficult. He had to get from the table-top and out of the skylight. Standing on the table he could just touch the ceiling. He needed more height. He looked round desperately. Had he slipped up? He thought for a moment. He would risk it. He took a bundle of the old newspapers from one of the racks and piled them on the table. When they came in the morning, they would take it that someone from the senior staff had been up looking for something. He took off his shoes, tied them with the laces round his neck, climbed up, and with an effort, for he was out of condition after months of sewing mailbags, pulled himself out on to the roof. Putting on his shoes again, he carefully shut the skylight, wiped the protruding hinges clear of the remains of the penetrating oil he had applied earlier, then rubbed some roof grime back across them. Only the closest inspection would reveal anything, and there was no reason for them to suspect. He rested briefly against a chimney stack and went through his actions once again, re-checking before it was too late. He had always been a careful operator. It had been others who had let him down in the past.

Along the roof tops to the next house, down the fire escape just as he had come. Half way to the bottom he spotted the policeman and froze, but when the officer looked up and saw him he merely signalled with his arm to some people sitting unseen in a nearby car. The man climbed to the ground, reaching it as they came towards him. What it was to be on the side of the law.

The Campsies, a range of green hills that stretch in an undulating belt to the north-west of Glasgow, had been chosen a few years earlier as the site of the main SBC transmitter mast. It was a powerful structure, linked to some efficient German-made equipment housed in a series of concrete buildings at its base. It beamed the Scottish Broadcasting Corporation's television programmes to the greater part of the central industrial belt.

At that time of night, about an hour after the man in gloves had come down from the Edinburgh roof, the little barbed wire compound that enclosed the station was abandoned to the mist. A couple of technicians came up the dirt track each day to check and overhaul, but otherwise it was more or less unattended. There was an efficient system of alarms to deter vandals, and on the few occasions when anything did go wrong with the highly automatic equipment, the mechanics could be up within minutes from their homes in the village down below.

Back to the uneventful life at the village station where a couple of drunks on a Saturday were the high spot of his week, PC Wraight, fresh from his ordeal at the riot amid the Glasgow slums, switched off the engine and jumped from the comparative warmth of his Land Rover. He produced a powerful torch and swung its beam back and forth across the high mesh fence and the gates of the compound. All seemed in perfect order. The garbled message, via the newsroom of the *Glasgow Herald,* tipping off the police about a threatened break-in, was obviously a load of rubbish. Except for children, there was little danger to the transmitter these days, ever since the new Broadcasting Protocol had been agreed allowing both political groups equal time to put their points of view on Television. A few years ago it had been different, and every transmitter in the country had been under constant military guard. Now, almost everyone had something to gain from free speech. Violence was confined to the city streets. The country at large was at peace.

Wraight went up to the gates and shook them vigorously. Everything was secure. A false alarm. He'd be able to go back now. His wife was waiting. He climbed into the Rover, switched on the two-way radio and put out his call sign. He told Control there was nothing amiss. Control came back straightaway about a second anonymous call to the *Herald.* They ordered him to do a further check. "Would you like assistance from Lennoxtown, ZF One?" the voice over the radio crackled.

"No need. ZF One. Over and out," Wraight replied irritably.

Back to the gate and then round the fence. The inspection

took only a few minutes. He stopped occasionally, peering through the slight mist, his torch beam cutting a reassuring swathe into the night. The windows of the huts were all firmly shut, and nothing, not even a rabbit, stirred.

At the Land Rover, he reported in again, but Control wasn't easily satisfied. He was told to wait and watch for half an hour, just to be on the safe side. Wraight asked them to let his wife know he'd be late, then switched off, looked at his watch, yawned and prepared to do his duty. Half an hour but not a minute more.

He gazed vacantly out of the windscreen. It had been an enormous relief to get away from his brief exposure to the filth, hate and violence of Glasgow. He liked the countryside, and had always been lucky to have escaped a posting to any of the big metropolitan forces. It was the friendliness of the people. They were kind, even to an Englishman like himself. It was only the climate that continued to depress him, after twenty years in exile. His roses fared worse than he did. He frequently told his wife that one day he'd go back home to Devon. There, a garden was a garden. . . .

PC Wraight didn't see the man in the blue duffle-coat run up to the fence at the far side of the compound. But he saw the burst of flame as the canister the man had lobbed hit the ground beside the tower. A bright, harmless flare lay burning among the sodden tufts of last year's grass. The policeman sat forward urgently in the driver's seat and seized the microphone. He gave his call sign, then briefly reported the fire. He told them he was going in to investigate.

Acting as it had been intended he should act, Wraight got out and went across to the gates. As he went he opened the sealed packet with the keys to the compound that were held for such an emergency by the policeman on duty. He found the Chubb that fitted the locks and swung the gates open. He ran across the compound towards the burning canister, and his sudden burst of speed caused the two men who were coming silently up behind him to misjudge their attack. One of them tripped slightly. Wraight heard them and turned. A brief hesitation, then they both came at him together. Instead of the silent knock-out blow that had been intended, there was a brief and vicious fight. The policeman broke away easily; he was much the fittest. He made for his Land Rover and the radio.

One of the men started to run after him. The other, a young, hard-faced man with sandy hair and a wisp of a beard, stayed still. He had something in his right hand. The noise of the shot was swallowed up by the surrounding mist before Police Constable Wraight's body had time to hit the turf. There was an ugly tear in the middle of the back of Wraight's uniform coat.

"You bloody lunatic. *Christ.* You've sodding done it now." The man who had started to chase the policeman had stopped in his tracks and, white in the face, was screaming at his colleague.

"Belt up will you," the younger man hissed back. "What's the Fuzz ever done for you? We've got work to do." The hardness of the voice killed further argument. The other man turned hesitantly and then walked quickly away out of the gate. In a moment or so he reappeared carrying a rucksack and a brown suitcase. They weighed a lot, and he had to rest once or twice. The other man made no move to help at first, then he moved forward, took the suitcase and the two men set off in silence towards the base of the transmitter.

Inside the Land Rover, Control's voice was crackling incessantly: "Come in ZF One. Come in ZF One. Are you receiving me? Repeat: Are you receiving me? Over."

Over in Lennoxtown ten miles away, Control had just put out a general alarm call when he heard the sound of the explosion.

FOUR

I AM NOT a family man. I have no children and might as well not have a wife. Angela had by reputation always had a good eye for a young politician on the way up, and, I had to admit, had chosen me rather than I her. For my part, I had mistaken physical desire, and a fascination for this woman whose name so frequently appeared in the society gossip columns, for love. We had both discovered our mistake in time to avoid having children.

I also have few friends. I am, I consider, a solitary person, genuinely preferring to spend the larger part of my time in my own company. I like to be on my own when I want to be on my own, and not when it suits other people. It is a matter of refusing, or rather being unwilling, to make the compromises necessary for friendship or family. Perhaps it's a weakness, but it's the way I am, and I am not afraid of it. What I do find less easy to bear is that I am too prone to be irritable and I suffer fools badly. I know people say simply that I am bad tempered. If I were not bad tempered I would be cold, and in consequence even more difficult to work with than I am at present.

Thus there was seldom pleasure in coming home. That night she was sitting in front of the television set in the small study of our official house in Charlotte Square. She smiled her usual martyred greeting, but her eyes were empty. Her elegantly thin face, which I had once found so attractive, formed those lines of bitchiness around the mouth which now symbolised her character to me.

I wheeled myself across the parquet to the open fire. She rose and pecked a dry kiss at my cheek, failed to make contact, but it hardly mattered. It was all part of a make-believe situation which she was careful enough to make formally correct. I was less anxious about appearances but was prepared to let things

ride, and as with Ingram, my driver, I seldom lost my temper
with her. It would have been pointless, since she had mobility,
and on occasions when I did get angry she would simply retire
to her upstairs room. We had recently converted the morning-
room on the ground floor into a bedroom to accommodate my
disability on one level. This was convenient to us both, and I
hadn't been upstairs since my return from hospital. I believe
she had had the rooms redecorated to her own peculiar taste,
but I could contain my curiosity to inspect them.

A rather too large whisky and then dinner. We had adopted
the habit, when eating alone, of reading during the meal, and
Angela had even had two rather neat mahogany book-rests
made to match the furniture. She had given me them amid
much public jollity at Christmas, while my present to her had
not stretched beyond the convenient cheque. I liked reading,
enjoyed the opportunity to relax, and it obviated the need for
us to talk to each other. The housekeeper, Ingram's wife, was
now used to serving us in total silence; we didn't even need to
ask each other for the salt, since a grateful constituent had
once presented me with two rather handsome Georgian silver
cruets.

The meal was mediocre and I drank more Beaujolais than I
should have wished to; it wasn't just to overwhelm the taste. I
had long suspected that there was an alcoholic inside me waiting
to break out. Angela was incensed by the cooking, however,
and broke the silence to announce, once again, that she would
give Mrs Ingram a week's notice. She always resolved to tell the
woman the following morning, by which time her mood had
usually passed. I said nothing and went on reading, which she
interpreted as my opposition to her plan for dismissing Mrs
Ingram. She was wrong; I was totally uninterested.

After a few moments Angela stood up and abruptly left the
table. She contained herself sufficiently to hesitate at the door
and claim that she had a headache, and for a moment I thought
she was going to stay. She seemed ill-at-ease, and I sensed that
there was something she wanted to say to me. But I was tired. I

remarked that she should see a doctor since her migraines seemed to time in so well with our eating alone together. This being hardly tactful in the circumstances, led to her slamming the door behind her, and my return to my peace, book and the wine.

Later I got Mrs Ingram to take a vacuum flask of coffee through to the study and asked her to leave the drinks tray in reach. I wheeled myself through to my desk; I intended to work and had asked Guthrie to send over the despatch box with my papers.

I poured myself a whisky without thinking, then left it untouched, since the Beaujolais was too much in evidence and I needed a fairly clear head. Once before I had had to tear up a lot of official papers which I had commented on while scarcely sober, and I was therefore well aware that my judgment could be considerably affected. I took the little key from my waistcoat pocket, unlocked the box, and had just begun leafing through my letters and files when the Duty Clerk at the Office rang to tell me about the explosion at the Campsie transmitter. He rang off immediately and I was gently puzzling over the implications when he rang again to tell me that a police officer had been killed. They had just found the body.

There followed an hour or so of intensive telephone discussions with a number of my senior advisers, the PM, and with a most indignant Police Commissioner. I worked the wine out of my system in the process, but balanced it out by attacking the whisky.

"I don't understand it," the Commissioner shouted at me across the wire. "Bloody political fanatics. I thought we'd have an end of this after the passage of your Broadcasting Protocol. You'll have to arm us now, Minister. The Force won't stand for much more of this, I can tell you. You'll have to . . ."

"We'll discuss it all at the National Security Committee tomorrow," I interrupted, equally angry. "I've arranged for it to meet at ten o'clock in the Main Operations Room. The PM says he may come himself. I would therefore be grateful for a full report by breakfast time at the latest. That's all. Goodnight, Commissioner. Goodnight." I abruptly slammed down the receiver to quell any further discussion. The whisky I had poured myself earlier had already gone and another one or two had followed it. I was not in an amiable mood.

Then the Controller of the SBC came on the line, a pretentious little man who, nonetheless, was quite able. He reported they had some low-power emergency transmitters working already, but that half the country had been affected. It would take at least three weeks till full power could be re-established. The situation was being considerably eased by the Bondi Corporation, the Bathgate-based telecommunications firm, who had offered the use of their own considerable transmission potential. They weren't even going to charge, the Controller added glibly.

"I don't trust charity when the State's the recipient," I said a trifle acidly. "What Government contract are they after?"

"None that I know of, Minister," came the slightly chastened reply. "They really are being *most* useful. We could hardly hope to function without them."

"I'll send a letter of thanks to their Chairman in the morning." As I spoke, I was aware that I was slurring my words, so after inviting the Controller to attend next morning's meeting, I hung up quickly. That would do for tonight.

I wheeled myself away from my desk and over to the fire. Out of habit, I poked the remaining embers as best as I could do from my chair, carefully placed the fire-guard in front, and after pouring myself a last drink, to help me sleep, went out of the room intending to go straight to bed.

The Charlotte Square house is well known as the official residence of the Minister of Home Affairs, and in the past there had always been a policeman on duty outside. It had been more a matter of prestige, and they had never bothered protecting me when I went to stay in our other house in the constituency. Since my accident the City Police had ironically and callously decided I was off the danger list in town as well, and the normal man on the beat had been considered sufficient to protect me. Not so tonight. The news of the explosion had travelled fast, and I noticed through the glass in the door that I now had two uniformed policemen outside.

In an alcove off the Adam hallway, a small, ugly internal switchboard had been installed, to Angela's disgust, to enable calls to be put through to any room in the house. On my way to my bedroom I stopped automatically to switch my line from the study to the instrument on my bedside table. As I did so, my wheelchair started rolling slightly, and by accident and helped by the drink, I must have pulled down the wrong lever, for when I got to my bedside and picked up the telephone to get a last check on developments from the Duty Officer, it was Angela's voice I heard. She was talking to someone in terms that were hardly open to misinterpretation. I didn't recognise the man's voice; he was being monosyllabic and much more discreet than my wife about the details of their obvious intimacy.

After a few moments my curiosity was overtaken more by disgust than by self-pity, and I quietly replaced the receiver. I wheeled myself back to the hall, flicked down the correct switch, and returned to my room. For the moment the whisky anaesthetised any dramatic feeling of betrayal at the evidence of my wife's unfaithfulness. I suppose I had been expecting it.

The phone rang again as I returned to my room. The Duty Officer was apologetic; there was something I ought to see at once. No, for security reasons, the papers had to remain in the office. They were sending a car for me.

The drive did wonders for my sobriety. By the time I got back to my office it was well after midnight, but the photographs which the Special Task Unit had enlarged were still damp. Each page of each letter in Torrance's file was there. It had been a neat job, quickly and expertly done, moral scruples set aside in the interests of the security of the State. I signed the hastily-drafted sentence-review which gave maximum remission to the safebreaker, wrote a Top Secret note to Guthrie, my Private Secretary, asking him to ensure that the warnings about talking already given to the safebreaker were repeated with sufficient threat behind them to ensure his total compliance. It would be disastrous if the operation were to leak, even though it would all be denied.

I settled down to study the papers. The most important document was a copy of a telegraphed despatch, dated some ten days previously. It was from Torrance to Liam MacPake, the ageing but far from elderly President of the Federation of American Caledonian Societies in New York. It gave the whole background to the approach Torrance had made to me. I began to read:

"The recent riots in Glasgow between the strikers and the Republicans, about which you will have had fairly full reports from my Deputy," Torrance began, "are brutal and much publicised incidents which demonstrate the bitterness and deep divisions existing in Scotland today. That several men have now died and many have been seriously injured, is a tragedy of sad dimensions, which could too easily prove to be a grim template for the future. While the short-term ability and willingness of the present Government and indeed of the great majority in the Scottish National Assembly to contain and defuse the present explosive situation is not immediately open to question, in the long run the serious economic climate with many more men unemployed than at any time since the 'thirties, a complete breakdown of collective bargaining in many of the most important sectors of the country's industry, and continuing balance of payments problems, must, if unchecked, lead to disaster. Even the expected boom in the North East, resulting from the vast discoveries of North Sea oil and gas, was a brief and shallow phenomenon. Once the capital work was done, the drillings made, the pipe-lines run ashore to Scotland and to the Continent, that was more or less the end of money flowing into Scottish pockets. That wealth now runs through Scotland as swiftly as the oil in the pipes, and all too little is diverted or available for local needs on the way.

"I am not dramatising the situation when I say that there are the makings of considerable and widespread civil strife in the air, out of which only those who seek to force the clock back to the days of the United Kingdom can hope to benefit. Many, too many, are already saying that independence was an expensive experiment that failed, and, significantly, they are speaking in the past tense. Support for the Reunionist Party is growing rapidly, and unless speedy and resolute action is taken, I cannot answer for the consequences. The Reunionists already have many of their members more or less overtly in the Government, in industry, the Civil Service and even in the Church. People who would be only too happy, for what they consider over-riding economic and political reasons, to return to the English or British fold. In this they assume, more than a little optimistically in my view, that they are wanted and would be welcomed back with open arms. England too has its immense problems, but conditions are in many ways much better south of Berwick, and it would be foolish to work in the belief that they would accept Scotland back, warts and all.

"Nor is this my own speculation alone. My recent discussions with Home Affairs Minister Malcolm Mockingham demonstrate that he is obviously extremely concerned about the situation. As you know, my assessment of him has not always been a favourable one, but though he appeared indecisive at times, I believe he always had the best interests of his country at heart. Since his injury, about which I reported in my letter of the seventeenth of October, he has visibly aged, but I think that the violence of the attack that caused it has left not only its mark of bitterness, but also a fire that was hidden or lacking in him earlier. Scotland may yet benefit from the crime of the man who will certainly be sentenced to many years of hard labour in Peterhead Jail.

"Mockingham as good as confirmed my own view that the present ills are not solely caused by the basic and inherent weaknessess in the Scottish economy but to a great extent by the fact that too many of those who control that economy are among the foremost supporters of Reunionism. Both through incompetence and by design, a wrecking game is being played. Reserve Bank Governor Campbell is, as you know, at the forefront of the Reunionists, and why the Government has kept him on in his present post I am at a loss to understand. I hinted as much to Mockingham, but with care, as they are all enormously touchy about any suggestion of us American-Scots appearing to meddle in or influence Scottish internal affairs— Mockingham admittedly less so than some.

"I must apologise for the length of this report, but I consider that it is one of the most important the incumbent of this office may ever have to write. My message is this: unless a massive inflow of funds becomes available to tide the Scottish Government over its immediate difficulties, Scotland as an independent nation could once again cease to exist. What I am calling for is a sort of mini-Marshall Plan, financial backing of the magnitude that American and World Jewry gives to the State of Israel. Thus could the nation survive.

"But if you believe that we in the Federation can raise, and should give such financial support, and at present I would hesitate to quote a figure, I would then strongly argue that we should not give blindly as, in fits of generous euphoria, we have tended to do in the past. It must not be presented as charity. It must not be charity. It should be tied securely, but secretly, to Scottish Governmental promises to rectify those inherent personnel weaknesses in the existing economic management of the country which I have already touched upon. How and when this should be done must obviously be the subject of careful study. There is little time to be lost, but if it is to be effective, we must choose our channels with care. It would be pointless and indeed counterproductive to go direct to the Prime Minister or the Financial Secretary with such an offer. We must prepare the ground first, otherwise it would become known within hours, and the opponents—those too proud to accept what they would consider to be charity and those who, for Reunionist reasons, would fear the return to stability that was being proffered—would be able to join in attacking it as a renewed form of American neo-colonialism and bribery.

"In conclusion, therefore, I propose, if you and the Executive agree, that I should be instructed to approach Mockingham again—he is, above all, honest—and ask his views on the proposition. Thereafter, perhaps you yourself could arrange a discreet meeting . . ."

I put the report aside and glanced hastily through the subsequent papers. There was a short reply from the States giving the go-ahead in remarkably casual terms. Torrance had also found it somewhat off-hand and had scribbled something to this effect on the margin of the cable. There was a final message from him reporting his conversation with me on the previous Saturday, and listing my questions. I had been right in believing I could have drafted it. The man's anxiety stood out starkly, as did his fear that the urgency of his previous message had not been fully understood by the Federation.

Putting down the photographs, I wheeled myself across to the cocktail cabinet. So that was all. It seemed straightforward enough, though I could see the dangers of the strings that Torrance had proposed attaching to the money. Doubtless the character sketch of me would give me something to think about later. I poured myself a large whisky, adding a touch of water from a carafe. My attention was very much elsewhere, my hands were shaking, and I spilled most of the water over my fingers and on to the carpet. I stared out at the night. To my surprise, it was snowing, the flakes briefly catching the light as they drifted past my window. From The Mound came the constant muffled swish of countless tyres on the quickly melting slush, a comforting sound broken only by the occasional bleat of a car's horn, and the distant whooping of a police car or ambulance.

I wheeled myself back to my desk and on an impulse picked up the telephone. Eventually a sleepy night operator answered.

"Get me Special Commissioner Torrance on the line," I said.

"Yes, Sir. But you . . . er . . . realise it's two in the morning." The woman's voice gave a hesitant warning.

"Hell. I'm sorry. Leave it." I put down the receiver feeling rather foolish. I was tired, and had a gigantic hangover in store for myself. I'd better go home.

FIVE

THE MAIN OPERATIONS ROOM had been carefully designed with an eye to security, the main feature being the total lack of windows. This was all very well except that there was a work-to-rule among electricity maintenance men, and the air-conditioning wasn't working. An emergency generator unfortunately provided us with sufficient light for the PM to decree that we should carry on and use the room as agreed.

I had the expected hangover and hadn't begun thinking of my private problems. The Police Commissioner's report had been enough to go on with. It arrived along with, and was as unwelcome as, Mrs Ingram's breakfast: pages of detail about the calibre of the bullet in the policeman's back, the type of explosive used, but nothing, not a single clue, as to who had done the job. The Republicans and the Reunionists were both quoted in the later editions of the morning papers with statements accusing each other; and later on, I was beseiged by reporters demanding my comments as I left the house to come to the meeting.

The mood in the room was one of puzzled irritation. Puzzlement, because Special Branch reports indicated that at least the leadership on both sides were genuine in their protestations of innocence. The irritation was provided by the heat, the stuffiness of the room and by the fact that the PM, who had eventually decided to chair the meeting himself, was at his most indecisive. The conjoint lack of facts and ventilation didn't stop him talking, and his long verbose bouts of speculation added considerably to a very long and trying situation. Even the Police Commissioner and the Controller of the SBC, who perhaps knew him less well than the rest of us, gradually lost their awe of being at a meeting with him, and joined in the general feeling of frustration.

As usual, just as the nadir had been reached, the Secretary to the Cabinet took over. He seemed to be the only one who could interrupt the long disconnected stream of words. I might have done it, but the PM wasn't an easy man to cut in on unscathed. He had a long memory.

"Then, if we accept that the leadership is blameless on both sides, Prime Minister, it's either a small, unknown faction in one or other organisation, or . . ." MacDowall hesitated, looking round to make sure he had everyone's attention, rather like my Latin Master used to do, "or, it's some third party who . . ."

"I can't believe the latter. We'd know about it," interrupted the Police Commissioner.

". . . who, unknown though it or they are at the moment," MacDowall went on as if he hadn't noticed, "may be sooner or later identifiable by their motive. Not many can hope to gain . . ."

"Anarchist? Individual crank?" This time it was the Prime Minister who interrupted.

"Too big a job for a single man, Sir," said the Police Commissioner, "and my Bomb Squad think it too expertly done for any of the Anarchist groups we know about."

"Nonetheless," I broke my silence, "it might be better if we hint to the press that some such group is suspected of being behind it."

"No foundation for that at all in the evidence," the Commissioner responded tartly.

"If the alternative is, as Sir Alexander MacDowall suggests, to blame one side or the other," I went on, "then we'll have them at each other's throats in no time at all. The silent majority won't stay silent if they don't get their television and radio back fairly soon. If we can't provide bread we must keep the circuses rolling." My references to the dangers of further riots by idle unemployed met with a positive response even from the Police Commissioner.

"Very well then," said the Prime Minister. "We are agreed

that that is the line the press spokesman is to adopt." He looked round happily at the sweltering members of the National Security Committee as if, having agreed a press line, the problem was now solved. The PM was never expert at dealing with credibility gaps, and I was sure I wasn't alone at that instant in thinking that it was time he went. He really was past it.

"And meanwhile, we ask the Police Commissioner to pursue the investigation with the greatest urgency," said MacDowall. He was making notes on a pad in front of him and didn't even look up as he spoke.

"Of course, of course," said the Prime Minister beaming at us all. "Now if you would excuse me, I must . . . Malcolm, would you mind carrying on and clearing up any of the little bits and pieces?" If I hadn't been so annoyed, his patronising glance as he addressed me would have made me embarrassed for him. Whatever else, there was a general soundless sigh of relief as he left the room.

The first of my little bits and pieces was to adjourn to a room with sufficient air in it. The move made, the pace of the meeting sharpened perceptibly. We reviewed the evidence properly, decided on future security measures, arranged for the widest possible investigations to be carried out and then discussed getting the SBC back in working order again.

"This offer of the Bondi Corporation. What do people think?" I asked.

The welcome was general and the possibility of their doing it in order to land themselves some contract from us was firmly dismissed. I still had an odd uneasy doubt at the back of my mind about using their facilities, but no one else seemed to share it. Then the Controller of the SBC announced, a trifle shamefacedly, that the operation was already under way. Their help would ensure that most people would be receiving TV programmes by the evening, and in any case, the three weeks' delay he had mentioned in getting the Campsie transmitter working again was apparently a highly optimistic estimate, since the German firm which manufactured much of the equipment was now dubious about such a speedy delivery date.

We left it at that and I adjourned the meeting. I wasn't particularly satisfied with what had been agreed, but we were still too much in the dark to do anything else. I put my papers away slowly, making a few notes as I did so, and consequently was almost the last to leave the room. As I was wheeling myself away, Sir Alexander MacDowall came up behind me.

"I wonder if we could have a quick word, Minister," he said.

"Of course. Shall I come to your room? It's on this floor isn't it? I don't have to go upstairs?"

He wheeled me along the corridor to his room. Like mine, it was one of the more pleasant in the building, with a panoramic view of the City skyline. The walls were lined with bookshelves filled with bound volumes of Hansard from pre-independence days, and the few new red bindings of the Scottish Assembly Proceedings.

A girl, seated in a deep leather armchair by the window, rose as we came into the room. Tall, dark, with a well-proportioned face, when she smiled, as she did then, she was also immediately attractive. She must have been in her late twenties.

"My daughter Ealasaid, Minister."

We muttered a few routine catch phrases, but shook hands firmly. She neither looked pitying nor did she, as so many did, studiously avoid looking down at my wheelchair as if it didn't exist. These were two gestures which so often followed introductions now and which I had grown to hate.

"I'm sorry to disturb you both, Minister," she said at once. "I'll come back later, father, when you're free. It's my job: I can't stand much more of it." She was talking to her father now as if I weren't there, and the smile had gone.

"Not now, Ealasaid," MacDowall said abruptly.

"Sorry, I'll wait outside." For a moment she had looked worried, then came another smile, tense and formal rather than happy, and she left us. I found myself staring rather too hard at the door through which she had disappeared.

MacDowall pushed his half-moon glasses a fraction higher up the bridge of his nose.

"Problems," he said as if to himself. It made him sound almost human. He turned suddenly and looked at me.

"Ealasaid gets *so* involved."

He went across and sat down at his desk without explaining further, his businesslike mask assumed once again. The personal glimpse had gone and I didn't press him.

"I don't like it, Minister," he said after a slight pause.

"Nor I," I responded.

"Oh, I'm not just stating the obvious. Despite what was said just now at the meeting, it's not the anarchists, nor—and this is more important—nor do I believe it's the Republicans or the Reunionists. They have nothing to gain. Neither of them have an interest in chaos at this juncture. The Republicans are still licking their wounds after the Glasgow riot and they know that the country's ills aren't going to be solved by acts like this."

"The Reunionists have everything in their favour if, on top of all the economic problems, violence blows up again. It's calculated to drive the electorate into wanting to put the clock right back. The mass of the public value their security too much." I wheeled my chair across the carpet to his desk.

"Normally I would agree. But not now. The leadership knows that the so-called peaceful forces of unemployment will do the job for them. This sort of outrage makes moderate Reunionist supporters, like Campbell, swing right out of sympathy with them. You know, that, Minister. Campbell and his ilk would have nothing to do with violence." Campbell was Governor of the Reserve Bank.

"Then . . . ?" I decided it was best to let him go on without interruption.

"Then it's some other group who have something to gain. And it's not the English. They have enough on their plates. So . . . so who might benefit, who might be persuaded to do something that might otherwise go against the grain by this sudden additional threat to our stability?" His words were delivered in a measured, staccato voice.

I became aware that the Secretary to the Cabinet was staring hard at me. Again I was reminded of my Latin Master discovering I had failed to do my prep. My hangover had vanished. And then I realised what MacDowall was getting at.

"You're not suggesting that Torrance and the Federation of American Caledonian Societies is behind it?"

"No, not exactly. Thank you for letting me have the photographs of Torrance's file, by the way. I read everything through first thing this morning. I hear you stayed up most of the night."

"The documents didn't take us very far, though it's useful to have the background to their approach to me about the aid. There was no hint in them about any more underhand ploy. It was a lot of effort and dirty work for nothing."

"Yes. But a negative report can be useful in clearing the air." MacDowall was staring at me over the top of his glasses. I felt slightly disconcerted not knowing what he was getting at. My hands shifted uneasily on the metal driving wheels of my chair.

"Accepted. So if it's not the Republicans nor the Reunionists, and, from the evidence it looks as if the Federation have nothing to do with it, who *was* behind blowing up the transmitter?" I turned my chair and looked out of the window.

"Look at it this way," MacDowall replied softly. "The police have nothing, not one single report, not one substantial clue. That, you'll agree, could be very significant in itself. Not one clue," he repeated. "No footprint, no traces of strange vehicles nor people in the area."

"Very expert . . . or an inside job?"

"In the police? No, that's out of the question."

We sat in silence for some time. The phone on his desk rang. Inevitably it was the Police Commissioner. MacDowall put him on to me. He told me that reports were coming in that the main North of Scotland transmitter on the Moray Firth coast had just shared the same fate as the Campsie one. It was too early to be sure, but so far there was no news of any casualties. There hadn't been any tip-offs to the press this time.

I put the phone down and related the news to MacDowall who took it impassively.

"Is there a Bondi Corporation transmitter near there too?" he asked suddenly. I looked across at him.

"You're joking," I said.

"Not joking, just curious. It can wait till later though."

He went across to a large and rather hideous Victorian cupboard that stood in one corner of the room, opened it and took out a bottle of whisky and two glasses. "You'll join me?" he asked. I nodded. The hair of the dog might help my headache. I thought MacDowall looked greyer than usual.

"I'm afraid that at Cabinet tomorrow, you'll be under pressure. They'll be back at wanting to arm the police again. I think we should prepare our ground a little, if you can stand it," MacDowall went on. I nodded wearily.

"There's one other thing, Minister. I think you should go to New York soon. Very soon. Perhaps even without waiting for the Federation's reply to your questions."

I must have looked totally bewildered, for he adopted a kindly, patient attitude and began to explain his understanding of what lay behind the explosions and what he believed was odd about the letters in Torrance's Top Secret file.

SIX

THE GROUND WAS frozen hard and the gravediggers had used a pickaxe to get through to the softer soil under the surface. It was one of the bleakest cemeteries imaginable, set half way up a hill and well away from the church through an unkempt wasteland of elder and silver birch trees. Above and beyond stretched the wet, heather-covered hills.

They had built a series of little ramps of soft wood over the drainage runnels on the long ash path to allow my wheelchair to be manœuvred in a reasonably dignified way down to the site. From one point of view at least, I was the guest of honour at the funeral.

I arrived as the cortège came into view. The coffin, draped in some sort of banner, was carried by six bareheaded policemen. Somewhere, out of sight, someone was beating a drum, and the sound, with a rather messy lack of timing, echoed dully among the gravestones. Some three hundred people, many of the men in police uniform, stood around the grave. The dead policeman's family and other immediate mourners, in a dark line along one side, and the minister in purple and black, at the head of the pit, his vestments fluttering in the wind. He looked flabby and pompous. It would be a pity if he were; funerals could be moving.

I came to a halt a respectful few yards away, the wheels resting against an edge of wet turf. Guthrie, with me for the whole day, bent down and needlessly applied the brake on my chair. It wouldn't move in the mud. I carefully adjusted the black tie I had just borrowed from Ingram. In the rush to be on time, my own had been left behind at the office.

I was there because Cabinet had decided that I should be. The Government must be represented at the funeral of the policeman shot in the back when the transmitter had gone up.

Cabinet had agreed it was essential for the waning morale of the force, quite apart from the propriety of the gesture. It showed everyone that we, the Government, were horrified at the outrage.

We weren't alone in seeing the necessity of being represented. Both Reunionists and Republicans were there in force, to show publicly that their hands were clean. I recognised several unusually subdued faces from each faction, ranged in orderly ranks behind the police contingents, at opposite sides of the grave. Their presence might lend credence to Special Branch reports that neither mob had anything to do with it. I dismissed the thought that one or other side could, as the Mafia were said to have done, be there simply to ensure that their victim was well and truly buried.

Floodlights glared in my face and the flash guns started. The newsreel cameramen and press photographers were focusing on me; they had seen the dramatic potential of me in my wheelchair as the coffin passed by. I was correct in assuming that various versions of a picture of the half-quick and the dead would be on all the front pages tomorrow morning, and so I looked suitably grim. In many ways I felt it.

The minister *was* flabby, pompous and indescribably smug. He waxed eloquent with all the dangerous awareness of his brief prominence. He departed from the funeral rite to harangue the crowd and, via the television cameras, the country at large, about his righteous horror. He managed to debase the occasion with his mixed metaphors and his mock passion. He was a spineless hawk looking for vengeance, imagining to himself that he was enflaming a similar feeling in his captive audience.

He turned more dangerous. I looked round at the faces of the people, all turned inwards to follow the man's words. Tense, highly charged faces, a few tears even in men's eyes. The minister was shouting that Police Constable Wraight would become a martyr on the road towards a return to sanity, discipline and moral responsibility. He spoke the phrase "vengeance is mine, saith the Lord". He was a real eye for an eye for an eye man, even if half the world ended up blind. He started talking about arming the police, saying how essential it now was. The Police Commissioner had more ammunition now. Perhaps he had arranged it. I felt sick.

The rain came suddenly, dampened down my anger and turned the minister from being the centre of my irritation into a pitiful and rather damp buffoon. By the end of the sermon, with the last post blown badly and inappropriately by some local territorial soldier, and dust shovelled down on dust, I even brought myself to shake his hand and mutter a few words of thanks for his services. He smiled back condescendingly and I turned my wheelchair abruptly away to avoid disturbing my short-lived tolerance.

The dead policeman's wife came up with a boy of about fifteen, the eldest child. Both were dry-eyed, stunned by the event. I shook hands with them in the rain, to the accompaniment of more camera flash guns. We spoke for a moment, formal, meaningless things. I was left with only an impression of two rather lost individuals, of the wife's parting, unbitter remark that her husband wasn't even Scottish, that it was her fault he had come north of the Border at all.

It was all over. The minister advanced on me again. I sensed he was going to offer me hospitality. Hissing to Guthrie to get us away, I shouted an abrupt goodbye that stopped the man in his tracks, and off we went up the long slope to the church and the car. The Police Commissioner appeared from nowhere. I had expected that he would be there. He started to praise the minister's sermon but I brushed him off as well. I knew exactly what he was going to say. Policemen's guns could wait another twenty-four hours.

The going was slow. Guthrie had produced an umbrella from somewhere, gallantly attempting to shield me from the now heavy rain at the same time as trying to push the chair. We evolved a system where I held it, partially sheltering us both, though Guthrie had to bow to keep under it. He had to put up

with a lot of chores like this and did them rather well, with
surprisingly good grace. A dark, cadaverous man of thirty-two,
the slightly off-putting first impressions concealed a genuine
shyness of character, but this was offset by a conscientious,
quietly efficient approach to his work. His immediate colleagues seemed to like him well enough and he was even
popular with the girls in the secretariat, as much, I believe, for
his occasional shafts of wry good humour and surprising lack
of pomposity as for any natural bachelor attraction. He had
entered the Civil Service later than most of his colleagues after
doing a doctorate in Company Financing at Harvard Business
School, but his real reputation in academic circles had been
made over an exposé he had written when still an under-
graduate, of corruption and incompetence at various well-
known seats of learning. Its success had undermined any
prospect of an academic career and as the world of business had
no real appeal to him, he said he found the Civil Service a good
second choice. In any event, I liked him and he was a first-class
Private Secretary.

Eventually I got back to the car a great deal drier than either
he or Ingram. Both struggled in the rain to collapse my wheelchair as its hinge mechanism had jammed, while I offered not
terribly welcome advice from the shelter of the back seat of
the Rover.

We drove off, Guthrie beside Ingram in the front, and were
passing the church through the crowds dispersing to their cars
and buses, when I saw Ealasaid MacDowall standing under the
partial shelter of a tree, the collar of her riding mac' turned up
against the rain. She was looking round anxiously. I motioned
Ingram to stop, wound the rear window down and shouted
across to ask if she wanted a lift anywhere. Startled for a
moment, she recognised me and smiled through the rain.

"I seem to have lost the rest of the team," she shouted back.
"They were in a large blue SBC van."

Then she noticed Guthrie. "Oh hello," she said in an
embarrassed sort of way. He smiled back shyly.

"Well, if we all know each other, can't we give you a lift?"
I said, surprised both that I wanted her to accept and also by my
sudden feeling of something, not far removed from jealousy,
that my Private Secretary should know her. She made that sort
of impact.

Darting across from her shelter, she got into the back of the
car beside me. "Thanks. Perhaps they thought I had gone back
in the producer's car or something, I'm a trainee Outside
Broadcasts producer with the SBC," she explained as an
afterthought.

"Not the most pleasant of assignments." I looked at her
closely.

"Terrible," she said, partially addressing Guthrie. "I hate it.
But they tell me one becomes hardened."

Ingram looked enquiringly over his shoulder. I realised that
we were still stationary, that he was waiting for my instructions.

"Edinburgh?" I asked the girl.

"Sorry. Yes, thank you very much."

Ingram gave an almost imperceptible shrug of amusement
in the direction of Guthrie, slipped into gear and we drove off.
Ealasaid MacDowall was looking across in my direction, and,
as we passed the last of the cars by the church, I failed to tell
her I had seen the blue SBC van standing by the kerb, the
driver outside looking anxiously about him, searching for
someone. I think Guthrie noticed, but he kept it to himself.

It was among the more pleasant drives I can remember,
though much too short. We were both seated, and therefore
my lack of worthwhile legs was not as obvious as usual. I
could forget. I'm not quite sure what we talked about except
that it was a relaxed and easy conversation, especially after
Guthrie had tactfully or calculatingly closed the glass partition
between us and the driving compartment. I hadn't deliberately
cut him out of the conversation, but it wasn't easy for him to
take part from where he was sitting. Only when we reached the
outskirts of Edinburgh and I focused on the silhouette of the
castle against the dark grey of the sky, did I hold myself in

check again, back away from the conversation, re-engage my defence mechanism. She was, after all, the first person I had talked to like that since my accident, and for a long time before that as well.

We dropped her at the west end of Princes Street. I knew my last few remarks and the goodbye were stilted and remote. She looked at me oddly for an instant as she got out, then smiled and I smiled back. She turned and walked away quickly and was out of sight almost before Ingram had turned the Rove into the stream of traffic again.

SEVEN

I'VE ALWAYS BEEN fascinated by the process of government by committee, and, in periods of less energetic intellectual thought, by the social behaviour of committee-men. Men with alert eyes, men asleep; men attentive, men simply appearing to be so. Little men, napoleons for the most part, peering precisely over the tops of their briefs; tall men lolling arrogant, effortless and casual across, rather than in, their chairs. All the mannerisms, subtleties and techniques of being a committee-man, of succeeding or failing; above all, the art of the chairman, of silencing the talkative without giving offence; of encouraging the vague and hesitant if it suits one's purpose, in order to coax the best advantage out of the gathering, rather than have to do with the lowest common denominator of available talent. I enjoy committees, especially when I am in control, when I can accelerate or brake the pace.

Where I have not been in the chair, as, for example, in Cabinet, I have attempted to develop a method of influencing decisions from less eminent positions along the edge of the green baize table. A carefully timed intervention can work marvels, even with an incoherent meeting and antagonistic chairman, and I would claim that I have frequent, modest success in this direction. But I admit I am no match for MacDowall, the Secretary to the Cabinet, who has taken this science to remarkable, and unless one finds oneself on the opposing side, to delightful, lengths with his ability to run the discussions of his nominally more senior and important fellow men. In this Cabinet at least, it was he rather than the Prime Minister who was *primus inter pares*.

The following morning's Cabinet discussions on the crisis were thus manipulated, as a result of my conspiring with MacDowall in advance. So, even if the Prime Minister's summing up of the discussion was not quite up to what we wanted, the Cabinet Minutes, initialled off in haste by a busy PM after a heavy lunch—and there is a sub-study to be done on the timing of such moves—had been meticulously drafted to our entire satisfaction. The relevant section read as follows:

"After lengthy discussion, Cabinet agreed unanimously that, while the security of the nation was obviously seriously at risk, until the source of the threat could be positively ascertained, there was no immediate value in rearming the police, placing the Army on special alert or calling out the Volunteer Reserve. This decision should be kept continually under review, but Cabinet unanimously decided that to take any of the measures mentioned above would only create wide-scale alarm and despondency among the population at large. This decision will, of course, not prejudice the existing authority of the Commissioner of Police to issue arms on a strictly limited basis to members of the constabulary for special operations. It was further agreed that the Commissioner of Police, the Head of Special Branch, and Heads of the other Departments concerned, would be required to meet daily under the Chairmanship of the Secretary to the Cabinet to keep the situation under review, and to co-ordinate efforts to track down the perpetrators of the two bombings. Cabinet agreed, finally, to accept the offer of the Bondi Corporation and use their North of Scotland transmitter at Elgin, as well as the one at Bathgate, to keep the Scottish Broadcasting Corporation's programmes on the air. The Secretary to the Cabinet is required to ensure that these decisions are carried out forthwith."

There had been the expected, very heated arguments about rearming. Dr MacKinnon accused me of catastrophic weakness and ridiculous optimism and stormed out of the meeting. I was far from worried by that demonstration since it made it all the easier to get it agreed that MacDowall, as Secretary to the Cabinet, should chair the daily meeting on security rather than myself. I left it to MacDowall to announce, in a very matter of fact way, that, in order to keep the temperature low and to ensure that there was nothing to suggest that the Government were rattled by the bombings, I should stick to my long-arranged engagement to travel to New York the following day, to call on the Secretary General of the United Nations and, incidentally, to meet the President of the Federation of American Caledonian Societies. There was scarcely a ripple of disagreement at this, despite the fact that it was news to everyone present that I had such a long-standing commitment. It was a further testimonial to the way MacDowall was able to manipulate things.

I rather suspected MacDowall had scarcely slept that night what with telephone calls and cables to New York resuscitating the genuine, but frequently postponed, invitation from the Secretary General. So often that is how Government works. It is entirely a matter of presentation, timing and of ensuring there is no credibility gap. Guthrie and two of my top permanent officials, the only other people apart from MacDowall who knew about my sudden change of plan—but not the full reason for it—were already hard at work in an effort to ensure that there should be no surprise in anyone's mind about my visit. Their own surprise I had taken care of with a hastily contrived story, backed up by MacDowall, that the meeting with the UN Secretary General was to forestall possible moves by England, among others, to get the Scottish internal situation discussed by the Security Council. A totally unfounded fear, but again a speedily contrived intelligence report from London saw to that as well. Make people partners to a deep conspiracy and they'll believe anything.

It was over ten days since I had overheard the telephone conversation which had revealed my wife's love-affair, a period in which I had seen her often enough, but during which I had made every effort never to be alone with her. It was easily done; there had been the dinner parties, a couple of receptions, but apart from that, I had been kept busy, working late, and we lived and slept completely apart in any case. She too had no reason for wishing it otherwise.

But there was an ominous gap for the evening ahead. I was leaving from Prestwick on the direct flight to New York at ten the following morning, and I was forced to go back to pack, and arrange my personal affairs. I could only hope she would be out on one pretext or another.

But when I arrived back at seven she was in the study watching some inane comedy programme on television. She complained about the reception and I explained sarcastically that, in case she hadn't heard, there had been two explosions which had wrecked the transmitters. She didn't react as badly as I had anticipated, but smiled and apologised for her stupidity. I wondered a little at that.

"Mrs Ingram's gone off for the evening," she announced, getting up and switching off the set. "I felt I was getting out of touch in the kitchen, so I've made our supper. It's been a long time." She smiled again, a fraction nervously, I thought.

"Yes," I said, wheeling myself over and helping myself to a drink from the cabinet. I had no wish to play happy families.

"Malcolm, I want to talk to you."

"Yes?" I repeated. It was the last thing I wanted to do.

"Please, it's important." The smile had disappeared.

I looked directly at her for the first time in months. "Well?" I asked woodenly.

"Could I have a drink too?" She was nervous. I poured her a whisky, and dropped two ice cubes into the tumbler. I wheeled myself over and handed it to her.

"Well?" I asked again after a few moments' pause.

"Malcolm, I'm leaving you."

"I see." I could hardly be surprised by her news. But she could have spared me the home cooking.

"Please, Malcolm, I want you to understand. It's not because of your . . . I would have gone long before this if it hadn't been for your accident. I felt sorry, genuinely. You must realise that." Her normally hard and bitchy face was softened and, to my surprise, I realised she was near to tears. Perhaps now that she had brought herself to speak to me, her words were more of a surprise to her than to me.

"I've hardly eaten since breakfast," I said flatly. "Can't we discuss this on full stomachs, then we'll be able to judge how lucky whichever man it is is going to be in terms of your culinary expertise."

She started to cry at that but I couldn't have cared less. I went through to the dining-room in silence and she followed lamely behind. In a way I was looking forward to things coming to a head.

The table was set for two and candles were burning in the middle. It was beyond me why she should have thought that such a homespun setting would help things along. Perhaps she was expecting it not so much to sweeten the pill as to make me realise how much I was going to miss her.

With Mrs. Ingram gone, she had to serve me, so the contact was even more unusual. She had gone to obvious trouble in the kitchen, the soufflé was excellent and she had rifled my wine cellar to good purpose. The mahogany book-rests were discreetly folded away on the sideboard.

The first half of the meal passed in silence. I worked my way through one bottle and opened another. Then she began talking, pouring it all out again, unasked. Apart from inserting a self-explanatory remark at the beginning to let her know that I had been aware of her affair for the past ten days, I didn't interrupt her. She went on about how much in love she was. She told me how it had started, she announced that she was going down to London to get away from me. The only thing she omitted was her lover's name, which made me suspect that I must know him.

After a while I stopped listening, but my total silence, far from disconcerting her, seemed to give her free rein. She went on and on in a torrent of self-justification. From time to time she repeated the phrase that it was nothing to do with me being a cripple. That at least registered with me; it obviously worried

her as well. Yet it left me distant, thinking of nothing in particular, though I half realised I would have to face up to the
implications later. I was off to New York in the morning and,
in the meantime, she could do what she liked, as she had always
done. I stared at my empty wineglass.

"Aren't you going to say anything, react, do something?"
I became aware that she was standing at her end of the table,
white and shaking, hands clenched by her side. Her voice had
become strident and unpleasant.

I shrugged. "What do you expect me to do? Burst into tears
or something? Sorry, Angela. I can't oblige you. Now if you
don't mind, and now you've got it all nicely off your chest, I
have some packing to do. You've probably done yours
already." I slowly swivelled my chair round, turning my back
on her.

I could sense she was still undecided and I waited, half
expecting another outburst. I wondered for an instant whether
she would throw a plate or something, but that would be very
much out of character. She had always been meticulously careful with our possessions. After a moment or two I heard her
leave the room. She didn't even bang the door.

I emptied the remains of the second bottle of wine into my
glass. It would help me sleep, something I never did before a
journey. Only then did I experience a brief bout of foiled
curiosity as to who the other man could be.

EIGHT

ON TRANSATLANTIC FLIGHTS, I alter my watch to the time at my destination point immediately I board the aircraft. Prestwick to Kennedy Airport is some seven hours flying time on the sort of sub-sound-barrier plane I prefer, seven hours in which to adjust my system to the change of timing and pace.

Like most long-haul flights these days, it was three-quarters empty, and I could spread myself across two First-Class seats. It seemed unfair since Guthrie was travelling tourist; although I managed to get him along with me, regulations applied even to Ministers' Private Secretaries, and forbade his travelling First, on economy grounds. He came through regularly every hour or so to make sure I was all right.

It was my first major journey since my accident. I had become used to short trips by car, the inconveniences of transferring myself in and out along with my wheelchair, but I had given little thought to the possible problems involved in air transport. Between them, Guthrie and the airline had worked it all out, however, and I was wheeled aboard along a telescopic boarding ramp, and my wheelchair was then folded away neatly in a convenient slot behind my seat.

The first hour or so I spent digesting the morning papers at leisure, a pleasant change from the five minutes flat I gave them in a normal day. They all made reference to my trip, mostly without comment. Only one was critical, suggesting I was turning my back on the crisis, hinting, though not in so many words, that I was past it, that a younger man might be brought in, to release me, as they put it, for a *less demanding* physical role. *Younger*—they confused age with infirmity since they must know I am only forty-two.

The brittle-looking stewardess offered me a late breakfast but I opted in favour of a couple of glasses of fresh orange juice. With the import surcharge we had had to introduce last year, oranges, along with most imported goods, were too expensive for that to be a frequent luxury. As I sipped it, I felt pleasantly relaxed despite the traumatic past few days, and by the time we were two hours out, the vibration and the sun streaming through the gaps in the drawn blinds of the cabin, had suspended me in an agreeable limbo into which my wife's imminent departure and the unreality of my mission scarcely intruded.

When I woke some time later the stewardess came up again and handed me a visiting card. William Torrance of the Federation was sitting further down the plane, and wondered if he could join me for a drink. I didn't feel like business, but I agreed, and she went off to get him. I could hardly snub him since it was his President I was going to see, and he was probably making the journey because of me, to brief his people in advance about what I was likely to say. I knew from his letters that his style of reporting was sensible and intelligent, and that he was on the right side of the fence. Admittedly some of the things he had said about me were not altogether calculated to endear him to me, but then he wasn't to know that I had seen his correspondence.

He came up at once, a large, jovial man with close-cropped, fiery red hair suggestive of his Celtic origins. A third-generation American and former insurance broker, he maintained some business connections on the side, despite his semi-official status as the Ambassador to Scotland of his fellow Scottish-Americans. Only his prominent chin and incipient jowls gave him away, a peculiarly American characteristic which I had always felt must be the result of a childhood where jaw muscles were over-developed by addiction to chewing gum.

We both rather self-consciously ordered Bourbon and ginger, a pleasant if slightly sickly drink totally unrelated to whisky, and then he began to talk. Not business at first but, inevitably, about golf, which, it appeared, was a major reason why William S. Torrance Jr had so gladly seized the offer of his present job. He also talked at length about his son, a student at New York State University, William Torrance the Third, who emerged from his father's description of him as the typical all-American boy, though also intelligent. I become restless when people insist on discussing their families. As I have said, I am not a family man.

Then, pleasantries, if one can call them such, over, he got down to it. He, if anyone, could have guessed the main reason for my visit, that it could only partially be to do with calling on the UN Secretary General, despite what the Secretary to the Cabinet had told him. My hurried change of plan must have made him think that my call on the President of his Federation was far from secondary. He must have suspected that he had sufficiently baited me with his offer of large-scale financial aid.

Torrance was cautious at first, and I stuck firmly to the line I had given him. But, as the journey progressed and a second and then a third drink appeared, he warmed up, became more open about how he saw such a gesture being presented to the National Assembly and to the public without giving rise to accusations of charity or bribery. I held back, letting him make the running, only prompting him from time to time to keep up the flow of confidences. In the end, however, he had no more ideas than I had already discarded as to a possible solution.

Then, more rewardingly, he turned to the latest developments; the blowing up of the two transmitters. I pressed for his assessment of who was responsible. Interestingly enough, he, too, said he believed that neither of the obvious candidates was to blame, which, if I hadn't already been convinced by the documentary evidence, would have confirmed my view that he at least was playing it straight. Had the Federation been in any way involved, had it been, as I had at one stage thought, some wild attempt by them to force my hand, then surely he would have gone to considerable lengths to convince me that the Reunionists or the extreme Republicans were to blame. I pressed him further.

He began to talk freely, by now slightly drunk. He must have had one or two before he had come to join me.

"In the strictest confidence," he said, "I'm extremely worried. That's not as obvious a remark as it might seem. Scotland's future is of great concern to me. I sometimes feel more loyalty to it than to my own employers. There . . . there is something going on which I don't like." His words were slurred.

"What d'you mean?" I asked patiently.

"We Americans pride ourselves, or at least we like to believe, we know as much about Scotland's economic and political prospects as you know yourselves. You'll admit it's often much easier for an outsider to look in."

I nodded slowly, anxious for him to get to the point.

"Yet I still end up puzzled," he went on. He sounded surprised and slightly hurt. "There is a new element which I haven't quite managed to isolate. There are a few straws in the wind; there were, even before the transmitters were blown up. Someone's out to cause trouble. I'd an unconfirmed report from a friend in the States that there's a small group being paid to work up discontent among our own members over there. I shouldn't be mentioning it, so please keep it strictly to yourself. I've some reason to think that one of that group was over in Scotland last week when the transmitters went up. Then I've some further evidence which suggests our Edinburgh Office was broken into; nothing appears to have gone, but there could have been an attempt to get at our papers."

The news about the group and the unwanted visitor to Scotland was distinctly interesting, just as his suspicions about the break-in were unwelcome.

"Why should any such group want to do this, and why should they be so interested in you?" I asked, hoping my biased interest didn't reveal itself. "What makes you suspect that someone has broken in?"

"Little things suggest an intruder. No fingermarks at all on the combination lock of my safe, a pile of newspapers in an attic room that looks as if it's been used as a stepping-stone, and the sudden departure of one of our clerks who could well have set the whole thing up." The last point was a new element to me, but I had guessed that my Special Task Unit must have employed inside help.

"Tell me more about this group. Who's behind them? What methods are they using to cause dissension?"

"I'm not fully in the picture, Minister. We've nothing definite to go on. MacPake, the President of the Federation, will probably give you more information when you see him tomorrow. But I'd be grateful if you didn't mention that I've already been filling you in about our suspicions. I'm exceeding my brief, and I think he may want to put you in the picture himself. By the way, while you'll also be meeting the full Federation Executive, he, MacPake, tells me he wants to see you on your own about one or two of the more sensitive points. There are wheels within wheels, you understand, and some of my reporting has only had limited circulation. I'm not sure how far the rot has spread."

I was about to press him further when the loudspeaker above our heads crackled and there was an announcement that we were running into a patch of bad weather. I had already noticed a few bumpy patches but when I turned towards Torrance again, I noticed that he was already looking green. He started to say something; then, with an abrupt apology about being a very poor traveller, he was up and away in a hectic dash for relief.

It really did begin to get bumpy and I felt sorry for Torrance who must now be having a rather hard time. The stewardess came up unsteadily and said that they were delaying serving lunch until we were through the turbulence, but in the meantime, would I like another drink? I felt I'd had quite enough even for me, and asked instead if they could produce me a cup of black coffee without too much difficulty.

She brought it to me a minute or so later, and was placing it gingerly on the folding tray in front of me just as the plane took a rather heavy knock. The scalding coffee inevitably slopped over and poured down on to my legs.

The stewardess rushed for a cloth. "Damn the clumsy idiot," I thought. "Aren't Hostesses meant to be trained to avoid things like that." Then suddenly I had to grit my teeth against the unexpected pain as the hot coffee seeped through my trousers.

On her return, the girl looked at me decidedly oddly, since I was now sitting and grinning like a mad thing. It hadn't been my imagination. I really had felt the pain in my legs. That must be a small sign of hope that they were not as completely dead as I had long believed.

NINE

As I HAD expected, my meeting with the UN Secretary General was brief, formal and inconclusive, as befitted an interview between him and a mere Minister of Home Affairs. Having rashly set aside up to an hour and a half for it on my programme, I had plenty of time on my hands before the lunch with the Federation Executive. The driver and the car they had kindly provided for me made me think about going, with Guthrie, on a brief tour of the sights, since I hadn't been there for a long time. But being a tourist in New York is frustrating at the best of times, and after a good half hour spent stuck in a traffic jam resulting from some political demonstrations and having moved only a block from the UN building, we abandoned the idea.

Consequently, as the traffic then miraculously cleared, I arrived at the Madison Avenue headquarters half an hour too early and had to put up with being entertained for much of the intervening time, if you can call it being entertained, by a Miss Matheson, an extremely acid Scots woman of about forty, who claimed to be MacPake's Personal Secretary. She spent the time, with what I later discovered was a most unusual bout of verbosity, in the national sport of running down America, Americans and all things American. She still retained a touch of upper-class Scottish accent in her clipped invective, despite her twenty years of exile from North Berwick. Guthrie had abandoned me at the door as he hadn't been invited to the lunch and had some friend from Harvard days that he was meeting up with, so I had no protection till McaPake and the others turned up. I shut my mind to the woman after the first few unnecessary pieces of bitterness, so, while she had me a captive audience in physical terms, my training in having lived with Angela over the years stood me in good stead.

Eventually the others arrived, the secretary lapsed into silent efficiency and produced excellent martinis as dry as her temperament, and we all sat round in MacPake's office for the next hour or so, before going through to his private dining-room for lunch. It's an odd American habit drinking lots beforehand then practically nothing but iced water with the meal, but I survived.

Apart from MacPake and Torrance, there were only three other members of the Executive there; Lindsay, Carlyle and de Laski, all of whom I had met at least once before in Scotland. The two other statutory members of the Executive were, as MacPake charitably put it, sleeping members, there because of their past generosity rather than for any present activity.

MacPake, a youthful sixty-five-year-old, was a highly successful real estate entrepreneur; a rich, gangling man who was just beginning to show signs of wear. But he was ageing gracefully, and I knew he still had all his wits about him. He sat swivelling back and forth in his black executive chair with a gusto that was more like a schoolboy's than that of director of Rubin, Corvo and MacPake Inc, and President of the Federation of American Caledonian Societies. He was totally honest and kind. I had had him to stay in Edinburgh when he first started coming over, but he and Angela hadn't got on, to put it mildly, and so he now opted for the George Hotel.

From the moment I had heard about the offer of assistance I had wondered whether the idea had come from MacPake himself. I had rather doubted it. He wasn't quite inspired enough to think up gestures like that. I knew from the letters in the Special Commissioner's file that the written idea had come from the Edinburgh office, but that wasn't entirely conclusive, and there was something about Torrance's original letter which suggested that it wasn't all his own. It's an old trick. If you are not the best person in the best position to influence all your colleagues to some course of action, then get someone else to do it for you. I wasn't actually saying that Torrance had been put up to it; but in normal circumstances a man in his position would be out of his depth in making such a far-reaching request without the certain knowledge that he'd get some backing.

MacPake sat on my left; on the other side of me was Lindsay, a mild, elegantly-dressed laird of a man, vague, bespectacled with a kindly exterior of the sort shared by MacPake. I could hardly take him seriously, at least not in the context of modern Scotland, since, despite his faultless Caledonian pedigree, he hailed from Alabama, and in that drawling, unattractive voice of his, he put forward some frighteningly odd views of a hard Victorian kind that suggested I could have little political sympathy with him. According to reports he was there as a very generous contributor to Federation funds.

Carlyle, sitting opposite me, was totally different, a hard-faced, brash, New York businessman with more apparent thrust than intellect. He was an unlikely bedfellow, and I had wondered as long as I had known him that he should ever do anything charitable and unpaid, such as was his work on the Executive. He didn't seem the type. I thought back for a moment to Torrance's remark about wheels within wheels. Then I recalled that friends of mine who had been more identified with whipping up support for Scottish independence in the United States than I had in the years immediately before the break-up of the United Kingdom, had told me that he had been invaluable then, and that it wasn't at all odd, since he had had a well-known and long-standing grudge against the English ever since a series of catastrophic business deals in London some ten years previously.

Finally, there was de Laski. He claimed that even the Maltese in him, which had left him with his unlikely name, stemmed from a long line of Glasgow ice-cream shop proprietors. The rest of his family had come from Inverness. He was small, dark and, he claimed, celtic-looking, though it too could have been Mediterranean; very incongruously he was a constant pipe smoker, with a penchant for entirely unsuitable ones of the drooping Sherlock Holmes variety. He was the most recent recruit to the Executive and hadn't come up the normal way through having been a president or office bearer of some affiliated society. He had suddenly appeared from nowhere with impeccable sponsors in the most unlikely places, and had been swept in unopposed.

In all, an odd lot, but it was an agreeable meal of the most opulent kind. They called it a working lunch, but while a lot of business was talked, and they gave their proposal slightly more precise terms of reference, I learnt little that was new and certainly was offered nothing that would make it easier for me to sell their idea of the aid to my colleagues. I did, however, hear the total figure they had in mind, and it made me sit up. That sort of money was the real thing, and I could appreciate, even without the details, that a boost of this sort, spread over several years, would bring the Scottish economy to its feet in a very significant way.

With the exception of MacPake, they all seemed unmoved by my concern about the mechanics of giving the money. Carlyle announced drily that it would all work itself out once we had agreed the matter in principle, and even Torrance whom, I knew, was well aware of the political realities of the situation, nodded his agreement. But he had a lot of prestige at stake in getting general agreement to the plan.

By the time they had finished spelling out their case we had reached the coffee stage, and there was a pause in which I realised they were all waiting for me to give my reaction. I began by rehearsing the difficulties as I saw them, the impossibility of steering a clear course between the Republicans and neo-Republicans such as Dr Mackinnon, and the Reunionists such as Ian Campbell of the Reserve Bank. I stressed that I named these two only for purposes of example. There were many others, I went on, in all walks of life, who would be only too eager to reap the political rewards of condemning such aid. Once again, I realised all I was doing was hedging, waiting until they came up with their particular, detailed scheme. Despite what they had said already, I felt that they must have something worked out.

Torrance broke in with some sympathetic remark about Ian Campbell's trouble-making potential, and it was then that I really began to notice the tension between the others in the room. There had been the odd signs before, nothing much, a fraction too many forced smiles and pointed remarks that might have been taken in unpleasant ways. I was to be forgiven if I hadn't read too much into such things; I was in a strange environment, and everyone was there for my benefit. I wasn't involved in their internal difficulties.

It was Carlyle who broke the balance with a brusque "That's enough, Torrance. We can cope with Mr Campbell. Now, if you don't mind, the Minister's speaking."

Torrance had again had a little too much to drink, failed to take the hint and went on "Sorry, Carlyle. You're right. I used to think until yesterday, Minister, that Ian Campbell was a problem; I reported back on these lines often enough. But don't worry," he smiled happily at me. "Since I spoke to you on the plane yesterday, things have become clear, easier. Don't you worry about Campbell. As Carlyle says, my colleagues have him all tied . . ."

"*Enough*, I said, Torrance." Carlyle almost shouted the words. I noticed there were bright spots of anger high on his cheek-bones. The others looked on, saying nothing. MacPake looked anxious.

Torrance paused briefly, but wasn't to be silenced. "Come off it, Carlyle," he said with a desperate grin. "You've got to be honest with the Minister. He'll understand what you're getting at sooner or later. You might as well own up now. He can only say no, like I did. I tell you, Minister . . ."

It was de Laski who interrupted this time. "If you've quite finished, would you now mind leaving the members of the Executive alone with the Minister, Torrance," he said quietly, removing his pipe from his mouth. His slow delivery didn't obscure the element of threat. MacPake sat white and silent. Lindsay looked startled; he was obviously totally out of the picture.

"I . . . er . . . You can't dismiss me like . . ." Torrance began again. He now was flushed and slightly nervous.

"*Out*," shouted Carlyle, and reluctantly Torrance rose from the table, excused himself surprisingly gracefully to me, and quietly left the room. There was an embarrassed silence for a moment and then MacPake said:

"I'm sorry about that, Minister. Torrance seems to have had a few too many martinis. He's been working too hard recently I dare say." The tension was high in the air. I nodded my sympathy.

"Out of practice with our hard American drinking habits," broke in de Laski. "It's one thing sipping a good malt whisky late of an evening . . ." Everyone laughed in relief and the tension was broken. And my brief spell of euphoria with it.

TEN

THERE IS A basic physical predicament in talking to someone in a wheelchair. I'm only too well aware of it. If the group you are in is larger than two, then those standing on their own feet are embarrassed because they either have to stoop slightly and talk down to the invalid at his level, deliberately bringing him into the conversation by addressing every remark to him; or, if they stand upright and address each other, they are equally ill-at-ease because, aware of their conversation going on at a level which the man in the wheelchair may not manage to hear, they worry about his face being in line with their navels. In consequence, the easy way out is taken and the invalid gets ignored, except by the socially-obliged host and a handful of others exuding charity and pity.

I tend, therefore, to avoid cocktail parties and receptions except when, as now, I am the guest of honour. In such circumstances I position myself strategically, near a wall and surrounded by chairs of chosen height. I hold court there, encouraging people to sit and talk. They welcome it, as it relieves them of the weight on their feet along with the responsibility of having to decide whether it is acceptable form to sit down at a cocktail party.

After the tension of the working lunch this particular function was good-humoured and pleasant. MacPake was an excellent host and had rounded up an agreeable company of American-Scots to meet me. There were the inevitable oddities at both ends of that spectrum; the over-dressed would-be Scottish chieftains in kilts, straight from their Texan cattle ranches or insurance companies, who would certainly have been more comfortable and presentable in stetsons or New England suiting. At the other end, a curious number of out-of-place, hard-headed business men, many of whom had genuine enough Scottish names, but with appearances more akin to a child's concept of a New York gang boss. There was even a negro who claimed a grandmother from Aberdeen. MacPake himself prattled on at my side full of remarks such as: "The secret of my position is that I've never really enjoyed whisky, but I have trained myself to call it that instead of Bourbon." Then he would roar with laughter and it would generally be echoed by his guests. He was obviously a popular host.

Despite all this sham, it was good-natured, and for once I was enjoying being the centre of attraction. I had put aside for the evening the problem of what to do about the aid, but I looked forward to going into the real detail, following up some of MacDowall's ideas with MacPake in the morning.

As the party progressed, however, I became a little detached and bored by lengthy arguments over the location of the forthcoming Alabama Burns Night celebrations which three of my current court were discussing in the chairs round me. My attention wandered to where Guthrie was engaged in deep conversation with a podgy little man in pebble glasses at the far side of the room. Guthrie looked worried as he listened. Then the fat man looked at his watch, said something to Guthrie and darted out of the room. Guthrie turned to look around as one does at a strange party when one is abandoned. He caught me watching him and for a moment I thought he looked almost embarrassed. He frowned and came quickly across to me. I excused myself from the Burns fanatics as Guthrie crouched down behind my chair and whispered in my ear: "A gossip journalist, you possibly saw me talking to him, has just told me that Torrance has been run over. He's in hospital, in a bad way."

"Oh my God. I noticed he wasn't here. How the hell did that man know? Do the others . . . ?"

"Saw it on the tapes and he came over to break the news. He wants an exclusive quote from MacPake and was on to me about getting your reactions too."

"How did it happen?" I began. But just at that moment

MacPake appeared looking rather white. He climbed up on the table and banged for silence.

"I have some very sad news for you," he announced quietly. "I have just heard that William Torrance, whom you all know well, has been involved in an accident and is now lying seriously injured in hospital. As you know he arrived only yesterday with Mr Minister Mockingham." MacPake held up his hands for silence as the shocked murmur went round the room.

"I am trying to find out more details now. There's nothing anyone can do. Please carry on and I'll let you all know as soon as I hear anything."

MacPake clambered down again and came towards me.

"May I say how very sorry I am," I began formally. "Perhaps we should go over to the hospital. Is there anything I can do?"

"I don't think so, Minister. They're going to telephone me as soon as there is any more definite news. But if you like, do go across. I'll get Carlyle or someone to go with you. I can't leave my guests at the moment."

"I think there is very little point in your going over, Minister." De Laski had come up beside us while we had been speaking. "He's unconscious, and they're not letting anyone near him at present. I feel it might just add to the strain."

I started to argue, then stopped. I didn't want to make a nuisance of myself, and in any case at that moment Guthrie came up again with the journalist. He was an unprepossessing little man, scruffily dressed and with revoltingly bad breath. He introduced himself as Walt Tesco representing some insignificant news agency, but reluctantly I agreed to talk to him. I can't quite remember what I said, but it was about the sort of natural feeling of shock at what had happened, and I made a lot of remarks about what a good friend of Scotland Torrance was. Half way through the interview MacPake stood up on his table again and announced that Torrance had died without regaining consciousness. Without thinking, I changed to talking in the past tense.

I asked Tesco if he knew how it had happened. He talked

about a car that hadn't stopped and had yet to be traced. It had happened about an hour before over on the fringes of Harlem. I wondered at that. I didn't know much about Torrance's private life but it was odd that he should have been so relatively far away when he should have already been at the Reception. My mind went back to the fuss at lunch and I wondered if he had been out drowning his sorrows ever since. It would more easily explain the accident if he had been drunk.

"Can I ask you, Mr Minister, off the record, if Mr Torrance was in the habit of hitting the bottle?" The directness of Tesco's question threw me off guard for a moment, particularly as it fitted in so closely with what I had been thinking.

"Not as far as I know. But I . . . er . . . I think that is hardly an appropriate or delicate question in the circumstances," I said sharply, indicating clearly that the interview was at an end. We were alone and Tesco persisted.

"Sorry, Minister. A bit blunt, but I'm afraid this is my bread and butter." Tesco was so short that even in my chair he didn't tower sufficiently above me, and a whiff of bad breath hit me as he spoke.

"Then your diet isn't to my taste. Now if you'd excuse me."

"OK by me." Tesco smiled in a bland, myopic way as he made to leave. "You may be interested to know," he lowered his voice briefly, "that they're putting it around that Mr Torrance was stoned when the hit-and-run driver got him. But I've got one witness already who is certain he was as sober as you or I. And I haven't even started trying to find out yet, Mr Minister." With that, Tesco turned on his heel and waddled pompously away.

I watched him go, trying to make sense of what he had said. I saw MacPake go up to him as he walked across the room and heard him ask whether he still wanted the interview. Obviously the reply was unsatisfactory, for MacPake shrugged in irritation as Tesco strutted on and out of the room.

For a few moments I was left on my own, then Lindsay and a number of other guests gathered around me again. Already they were full of talk about collections for wreaths and the organisation of the funeral service. Someone asked if I could stay for it if they arranged it as early as possible. Their instant detachment sickened me and I gave curt, noncommittal answers, before excusing myself and wheeling over to where Guthrie was standing alone in a corner. Despite myself I found myself talking in the same sort of way.

"Do a draft of a telegram to the Prime Minister—reporting Torrance's death, will you, Guthrie, and then send another one, couched in suitable terms, from me to his wife. I believe MacPake has already broken it to her on the phone, poor woman. Come back immediately you've finished. I want to get away from this party as soon as possible. We'll have to decide whether I stay on here for the funeral. I expect the PM will want me to, and Treasury will be sure to back him up since it will cost them less than sending someone else over." Guthrie nodded and disappeared on his mission. I took another whisky from one of the waiters and prepared for a final half hour of being sociable. I wasn't looking forward to it. I wanted peace to think.

When the curtain came down for the interval, I realised I had appreciated little of the first half of the play. It was one of these unnecessarily brutal plots about a negro youth's struggle in a corrupt world. The director and author had, between them, taken every liberty which current permissiveness allowed.

While I had no composite reaction to it as a play, I was left with lots of vivid enough images of naked men and women copulating without feeling in a setting of violence and sadism.

It was the evening following the Reception. I sat alone, wheelchair drawn up level with the front row of the stalls; the end seat beside me was empty. MacPake had invited me, but at the last moment his driver arrived to deliver me to the theatre with the message that he had had to go off on some unexpected business. The suggestion had been made that one of his deputies accompany me in his stead, but I had resisted the prospect of some unwilling escort. MacPake had arranged for his driver to return and pick me up later. Unable to get to the bar during the interval I did what I never do and bought myself an ice cream from one of the attendants. I sat spooning it into my mouth as, once again, I reviewed the oddities of the day. I had had the promised lengthy session with MacPake this morning but it had been far from successful.

When I arrived at ten o'clock, de Laski was with MacPake in his office and I sensed some sort of row had been going on, though they both greeted me warmly. From the outset, MacPake appeared very shaken and upset by Torrance's death, but I read something more into his obvious deep anxiety. We settled down over coffee and it became rapidly apparent that de Laski intended to stay with us. After I had dropped a few hints and MacPake had pointedly ignored them, I came to realise that it was de Laski more than MacPake who was in charge. But I persisted and after a while, when I had made it obvious that I wasn't going to get down to business so long as de Laski remained, he reluctantly withdrew, saying, as he left, that the Executive would look forward to a full report on our talk as soon as possible. He took his drooping pipe out of his mouth and smiled as he said it, but I sensed that it was an order rather than a request to the Chairman of the Federation.

De Laski's departure produced little change and MacPake remained silent and withdrawn. I told him bluntly that I hadn't flown to New York for nothing, and thereafter he tried to pull himself together, apologising for his detachment by referring once again to Torrance.

But he still was untypically reticent and unforthcoming, and I determined to force him out of his silence by putting all my cards on the table. I again gave him the familiar background—the state of the Scottish economy, how Sir Alexander Mac-Dowall and I were worried about the implications of the latest bomb explosions—and I repeated how difficult it would be to sell to the Prime Minister and the Government their idea of financial aid. He listened to me in total silence. When I turned brazenly to begin voicing our suspicions about who might be behind deliberate fermentation of discontent in the country, I realised that he had stopped listening, and was scribbling on a pad in front of him. He slipped the paper to me, at the same time inserting some vague comment about how interesting my views were, to cover up the surprised hesitation in my voice.

The note read: *Keep talking. We may be being overheard so keep any delicate discussion till later. Will explain then.*

From then on, after I got over my startled amazement and initial assumption that MacPake had suddenly gone a bit mad, we talked in generalities. He responded glumly and we ended up, yet again, with nothing decided. After that I had gone back to my hotel and had spent the entire afternoon in bed, conserving my strength for the evening, and, I hoped, a more useful private talk with MacPake, in an attempt to get to the bottom of what was becoming more and more an extraordinary situation.

Looking back, it was inevitable that he wouldn't turn up. Someone, and presumably it was de Laski, was successfully preventing us from getting together privately. Was he worried that MacPake would tell me something he should not? How did this fit in with what Torrance had blurted out? What was the significance of the journalist Tesco's remark yesterday? My conjecturing was becoming ridiculously unreal; I found it beyond me to begin to understand what it all meant, and the strain of living in New York was beginning to tell heavily on me. I was permanently tired, I had been drinking too much and too often, and, as a result, I had an almost permanent headache. On top of it all, the pain I had felt in my leg and which I had greeted with so much joy on the aeroplane, had been replaced by something which had become more or less permanent. Not a violent pain, but a constant, evenly nagging pain, totally unconnected with the spilled coffee. I presumed it was some localised nervous system reawakening, and looked forward to talking to my doctor about it. I wasn't prepared to consult anyone here about it and, in consequence, I made do with lots of aspirin to kill the pain and allow me to sleep. It was an additional excuse to drink.

I was now eating an ice cream, and found it surprisingly agreeable. I ate it slowly, spinning it out till the curtain would rise again. I was deep in my thoughts and it took a little time to focus on the fact that someone had slipped into MacPake's empty seat beside me. I swivelled round enquiringly.

"Good evening, Minister. Can I join you for a moment or is the seat taken?" Ealasaid MacDowall was sitting smiling at me. It was the first pleasant thing that had happened to me in days, yet I only succeeded in muttering my surprise and delight at seeing her so unexpectedly.

"I'm over on what should be called a swan," she explained. "The new direct flight from Edinburgh was inaugurated yesterday and the airline have given a hundred of us journalists an opportunity of publicising it. I don't usually do this sort of thing, but my boss has just had a row with the management and resigned in a huff, so I willingly stepped into his shoes to savour the pleasures of transatlantic living."

"How clever to have spotted me. Are you here on your own?" I asked hopefully.

"The theatre? No. I'm with a couple of friends. And as to seeing you, well, you stand out. . . ."

"The wheelchair?"

"Yes. But I have an eye for picking out people I know in a crowd. My father has the same ability. He can spot a friend among thousands at a rugby international."

A bell rang in the foyer signalling the end of the interval. "I must get back," she said as the house lights began to fade.

"Please stay. I'd like you to," I said on an impulse and immediately felt embarrassed. I mustn't keep her from her friends. And she would stay too if I asked, out of kindness. "No, I'm sorry," I went on. "That's very selfish of me. Perhaps after . . ."

"Shh . . ." she said, taking my hand naturally as if to stifle my protested rethink, and she was still seated when the lights went out. It was only when the curtain rose to a new cacophony of sound and movement that we let each others' hands go. On my part the separation was reluctant.

The second half of the play degenerated even further, the participants replacing any residual talent with ridiculous obscenity. I am not prudish and am all in favour of orgies in their place, but not ones lacking taste and ability. It was like a bad sex film; ham acting, no conception of eroticism that must, above all, be subtle. Pornography would catch on if it were of a higher, more enlightened standard.

I welcomed the final curtain with relief and anticipation. During the most tedious parts of the last scene I had decided to ask Ealasaid to have dinner with me afterwards, in the expectation that I would almost certainly be refused and, if accepted, would be building up a store of problems for myself. In such circumstances one seldom acts rationally.

My invitation was accepted with what, even allowing for my understandably pessimistic approach, seemed quite genuine pleasure, and she disappeared to make her explanations to the friends who had brought her to the theatre. I gathered later that they were distant relatives of her mother's and that she was only too glad to get away from them. I didn't question her on her excuse.

MacPake's driver turned up as promised and I got him to drive us both to the only restaurant I knew where my wheel-chair would be easily manipulated. It was a spacious, old-fashioned place with dining cubicles along the walls and subdued lighting. As we entered I hoped Ealasaid didn't feel I had chosen too romantic a setting.

If she had her doubts she gave no sign of it. I held off the drink, though my legs were hurting, and our conversation became easy and far-flung. Towards the end I began to retrack, holding back, knowing that to do otherwise would get me hurt. A physical vegetable, I had to retain some protection for my emotional self.

I liked Ealasaid all the more because she realised it. She knew at once when I started with my withdrawal symptoms. But instead of accepting them, ignoring them or being upset by them, she challenged them. I found it impossible to respond, and after a while she gave up. I knew what was happening, but I couldn't help wondering what prompted her to pay me so much attention, she an attractive lively girl, me a crippled, bitter man a dozen years older than her, partially married on top of everything else. As a result I became reserved, distant, and I hated myself for it. I watched her become puzzled and then withdrawn in turn. I wanted to tell her why, but in the end I couldn't. I became tired, ordered and drank too large a brandy, and the evening ended disastrously with her having to see me back to my hotel in a taxi. I can remember her looking at me sadly as she left, with me being wheeled away to my room by the night porter. It had started so well.

ELEVEN

I COULD FEEL the rubber sheet under me. Why the hell did they still do it? I had perfect control over my bladder and it was degrading, apart from the discomfort. I'd bribe Sister Rogers.

But the little private room was cheerful, overlooking a pleasant stretch of gardens. There were vases of flowers everywhere, though I had tried to keep my return to hospital as close a secret as possible.

I had come in that morning. It was the first, long-arranged return since my convalescence after the accident. To all intents and purposes, it was a routine check-up, but Professor Taller of the Faculty of Medicine, my surgeon, had much more in view. He had put it to me gently the previous week, after I had told him about the constant pains in my legs, the renewal of feeling I had discovered when I had had the hot coffee spilled over me. It was a long, highly technical explanation based on numerous tests he had subsequently conducted on me. It was to involve an operation. He was open about it: it offered a fifty per cent chance of eventually seeing me get out of the wheelchair, but it involved a deal of pain and the possibility that, at the end, I might be much worse off. If the plates that were to be inserted were rejected by some part of my spine, then I might have a future where my back had to be supported in a permanent splint as well as being in a wheelchair. It was a two-stage operation, this the shorter and less complex part. I'd be out of circulation for three weeks to a month, and as the National Assembly was in recess it was an opportune moment if any was. I agreed, but only once I was as sure as I possibly could be that there would be no moves by the Prime Minister, inspired by my opponents within the party, to secure my retirement while I was out of the way. There had been attempts in the past, since there were several with their eyes on my job; but I now agreed to come into hospital in the confidence that I could rally support against any such move in the Assembly, the Cabinet, and in the country at large. I felt that it wouldn't need much background briefing by me to a few well-chosen journalists to ensure that any such move would be defeated by a popular outcry against me being removed while I was defenceless.

Sister Rogers, a pretty little nurse with a soft West Highland accent, came in with tea and a pile of letters and telegrams. So much for secrecy. I lay back against the pillows and began to go through them. Mainly from colleagues, and constituency workers, but there were a few from members of the public as well. Guthrie would arrange for acknowledgements to be sent out in the morning. One, only one, was from a crank, full of wild hatred and abuse. It didn't disturb me. People outside public life fail to realise how many anonymous, abusive, often obscene letters public figures earn, and how quickly one becomes immune.

It was a week since I left New York, only a week since Torrance's funeral with all its attendant ceremony. It had been impressive, and thousands had packed in the Scottish Church to pay their last respects. The police had failed to trace the driver of the car, but no one expected that particular line of enquiry to be pursued too hard since it had become pretty well generally accepted that Torrance had been up to his eyeballs when he had been hit. I for one had no reason to doubt it, since, despite what the journalist Tesco had told me, I remembered only too clearly Torrance's lunchtime outburst.

Following my evening at the theatre with Ealasaid, I considered the whole New York visit to have been a complete waste of time. I had no further opportunity to discuss things privately with MacPake, and though I saw him several more times, it was always in company with the others, and he made no move to take any initiative on his own account. I didn't read any sinister motive into it, despite the all-pervasive presence of de Laski and Carlyle, other than to put it down to a struggle for power within the Federation and a desire to keep decision-making in the corporate hands of the Executive. In the end I left saying that I would consider their offer further once I had worked out the modalities of selling it.

Nor did I see Ealasaid again, though I could have traced her had I felt sure enough of myself. I spent most of the rest of the time in my hotel room reading and waiting for the funeral, fully prepared to leave the moment it was over. I got some books from the University Library and read up on some of the pre-Adam Smith Scottish economists for a study I hoped to do some time on one of them; but I didn't get very far. I gave Guthrie leave to go and visit friends at Harvard, so I was totally on my own for several days. It was good in terms of relaxation, but I had much to worry about and my legs were giving me a lot of pain. I took to drinking on my own. It would have been really serious if I had had that opportunity for more than a few days.

And now I was back, waiting for the operation. In the meantime there had been a long and fruitless clearing of the air with MacDowall. Again we got nowhere. As with the latest trade and employment figures and the bomb outrages, we took the easy way and decided there would be no harm in letting things ride for a bit. We were also waiting to see whom the Federation would select to replace Torrance as Special Commissioner.

A knock at the door of my room and Guthrie came in bringing more letters and a red despatch box stuffed with official papers. My operation now wasn't until nine the next morning and I resolved to work to the last moment.

"How are you feeling, Minister?" he asked politely.

"Fine, apart from the bloody rubber sheet. But the operation's not until tomorrow. Ask me after that," I smiled.

Guthrie put the box down on my bedside table. He looked worried.

"What's the matter?" I asked jokingly. "Hangover or a lover's quarrel?"

"Well, nothing exactly, Minister, except that . . ." He

hesitated. I suppose I wasn't very forthcoming, so he didn't go on.

We had a few minutes' discussion over routine Ministry matters and then he said: "I've gone through your despatch box as usual, Minister, and sorted it into some degree of order. I read that report you asked for from Mr Matthews at the Department of Trade. It's very worrying." He hesitated again.

"Is it? Well I'll read it sometime." I paused "What's biting you, for goodness sake, Guthrie?" I barked. I hadn't seen him acting like this before.

"I'm sorry, Sir. It was that report. It reminded me of something I'd heard. But it's nothing important." Abruptly and expertly he changed the subject and I forgot about his bout of uncharacteristic anxiety. We went on with a number of other matters, I told him how I would like certain letters handled and so on, and then, after wishing me the best for my operation, he left again almost immediately with a batch of correspondence to reply to. I settled back in bed to do some reading.

I opened the box and glanced quickly through the papers I'd been sent. There were the usual routine submissions and requests from my officials asking for Ministerial approval for decisions they had, in the most part, already taken. I put them aside for the moment and took out the paper Guthrie had mentioned, a thick memorandum addressed to me from my colleague Matthews, the Minister of Trade. I had been worrying that while the short-term economic picture was not too bad, the long-term trends were far from encouraging. From the memorandum the permanent officials in the Department of Trade and Industrial Development were worried too. I had been seeing plenty of evidence in the growing concern at the rate not only at which we were getting into severe balance of payments difficulties but also the rate at which our larger firms and industries were being taken over by foreign based companies. It was, at first glance, a natural development in our reduced circumstances for Scottish owners to sell out for cash to whoever came along. I am far from being a narrow nationalist and appreciate that the international company has long flourished and will continue to prosper. No country can ever hope to be entirely independent economically or financially. All the Cassandra-type warnings and Gaullist anxieties about foreign economic domination will never have much effect in Western economies where money always goes where it can obtain the highest return. Yet setting this all aside, I had the feeling that this particular tide was flowing faster than was natural; so I had asked Matthews and his Department to let me have a breakdown of foreign-owned companies. It was this memorandum that had now been sent to me. An economist by training, I turned first to the statistics at the appendix. Statistics can easily be made to lie, but not quite as easily as the conclusions drawn from them.

I suppose I had realised it, but it was with fascination if not horror that I noted just how much my suspicions were justified, how many of our basic and advanced industries were now under mainly American control or ownership. This was additional to the well-publicised transatlantic interest in much of the country's press, and the pre-eminent relationship, of a very much one-sided nature, between certain American-based finance houses and our two major commercial banks.

It was no new development, this American investment in Scotland, and it had been of overwhelming benefit to us in the past. I was the first to admit that, without it, without the impetus this enormous dollar inflow had given us, we would never have had the nerve or strength to seize the opportunity of independence. But assistance and confidence in us as a buoyant, potential growth area was one thing; dollars buying us up wholesale when we were at rock bottom was another.

I spent about an hour on the paper, leaving the conclusions till last, and the latter set my mind somewhat at rest. The figures were alarming, but the conclusions stressed the contextual setting, and were both cautious and reassuring. I felt relieved that my anxieties were less well founded than I had expected. The doctor had been injecting me with some sort of drug prior to my operation and I was prepared to believe that this was affecting my judgment. Still, the figures were there and I would keep an eye on developments when I came out of hospital again. Matthews, the Minister responsible, wasn't the brightest or most alert of men, and he wouldn't notice a thing unless it were forced to his attention.

I lay back and shut my eyes. Perhaps I slept. When I opened them again, Ealasaid MacDowall was in the room. I sat up in pleasure.

"I thought I wasn't allowed any visitors," I smiled.

"I was at school with Sister Rogers. She said that if you didn't mind, she'd look the other way. Do you?"

"What do you think? I'm delighted to see you."

"I've brought you some flowers, but you seem to have plenty already." She looked round the room approvingly.

"It was meant to be a secret."

"Father mentioned something at breakfast this morning and I came round on the off-chance of being able to see you. I thought they might have operated on you straight away."

"No such luck. They always want you twenty-four hours in advance to fatten you up, test you and the like. But don't let's talk about it. When did you get back from the States?"

"Only yesterday. One thing led to another. They tried hard to get me to stay. I've had two or three offers of jobs."

"I'm glad you came back."

"Oh it's not settled yet. There's one tempting offer still very much in hand. That was one of the things I came round hoping to talk to you about. Oh I know it's very unthinking of me. There you are waiting to be cut up and I come along and start trying to burden you with my worries and suspicions."

"What are you talking about? You're bringing me in half way through like a story in a woman's magazine."

"And there's also the fact that you're an important man, a senior Minister. My father would be very angry if he knew."

"Of course, of course, and you're such a nonentity. You're beginning to sound like one of the characters in these woman's magazine stories, complete with all the apologies," I started to joke; then I appreciated she was looking far from happy.

She drew up a chair beside my bed, sat down determinedly and said, "All right. D'you mind? I'll begin at the beginning— God, you're right, only I now sound more like I'm beginning a bedtime story." I said nothing, lay back and waited, watching her uncertainty with growing puzzlement.

"There are three things," she began. "I didn't know who else to talk to about them, and it occurred to me that since you've just come back from the States too, having met some of the people involved, that you might begin to understand. I would have gone to my father but he'd think I was imagining things." As she spoke, she fiddled nervously with the handle of her handbag. Without interrupting, I reached over and took her hand to steady her. She seized my hand and held it tightly, but went on talking, as if nothing had happened.

"First of all, there's the job. Someone is trying to buy me. It came from some of the people I met at the Federation party. There's a man called de Laski. When he rang me up, I did a quick calculation as to whether, when he offered me this job, he was simply skirt-chasing, but I decided against it. He was serious. It's a magnificently paid job here in Scotland working as chief public relations officer for a telecommunications organisation, of which he's a Director, called the Bondi Corporation. Bondi is part of some enormous combine of the same name with its headquarters in Dallas, Texas."

"I know a bit about them," I said. "They've helped us a lot since the two transmitters were blown up. But that doesn't sound very odd to me. It suggests that you should be flattered, or that someone has at least seen your true worth," I added. My smile camouflaged a sudden concern.

Ealasaid looked grim. "Big business doesn't work that way. Not firms like that at any rate. They don't pick people like me, right out of a different league as it were, unless someone is desperately wanting to sleep with me or because I have something else they want."

I thought of a flippant remark, but instead decided to treat her as seriously as I felt. "Perhaps they want to get through to your father . . ." I began.

"I thought of that," she said immediately. "I've had a certain amount of that sort of thing in the past, people seeking me out as a way to get preferment from father. There'll always be people who take you on because of your important connections. It may just be true in this case too. But the important thing about this offer was not so much the motive as the way in which I was pursued. It wasn't the usual casual offer of a job. People kept ringing me up, producing written contracts, getting at me to make up my mind. They came at me from several directions at once. It's definitely me they're after and I don't think I'm too flattered by it. De Laski's even been on to personal friends of mine through other contacts of his, to try to persuade me to accept. But precisely why am I so important? It can't be my father alone. I don't have that much of a hold over him."

"Have you told him?"

"Not yet, as I said. I didn't want to involve him. He's a very matter-of-fact person and there may, after all, be nothing much in it. Perhaps this de Laski man really does want to sleep with me." She grinned thinly.

"I'm flattered you're telling me. But I think you underestimate your father. You told me there were three things?" I turned over on my side to be able to watch her better, and managed to do so without letting go of her hand.

"Yes. You came across a fellow, a journalist called Tesco."

"A myopic, evil-smelling, fat little man?"

"Oh he's not that bad. He's certainly kind. Well he found out who I was and came round with a story he had that Torrance, the former Federation man here . . . well, it sounds a bit far-fetched, but that he was bumped off. Tesco said there was evidence that it wasn't an accident, and he proved one thing to me. Torrance wasn't drunk when he was run over."

"Tesco started telling me something similar. There are cranks everywhere. Torrance was certainly well on the way to being plastered at lunchtime," I said. "I have the evidence of my own eyes for that."

"That's as maybe," Ealasaid responded. "But when he left the lunch he went straight for a sauna and massage, and then spent the next hour or so swimming. I met his son who swears blind that his father was sober, and he wasn't just saying so because it was his father. Torrance is on record as saying he was out to clear his head. When he left the health clinic the manager says he was as sober as you or I are now."

"Anyway, even if true, how does it lead this man Tesco to his weird conclusion that it wasn't an accident?"

"Because, for one thing, a lot of people have since gone to a lot of trouble to say that he was drunk. But the car that knocked him over climbed on to the pavement to do its work, so there was no question of Torrance wandering about on the open street, and the car and driver not yet traced of course, drove fast and skilfully away after its finely executed manœuvre. Tesco took me to an eyewitness who swore it was deliberate. Funny thing was when we came back the next day to take a verbatim record from him, he had disappeared from his usual haunts and when we finally tracked him down he retracted everything he had said earlier. The man was scared stiff. He had so obviously been warned off."

"That sounds a bit dramatic," I said quietly, patting her captive hand gently.

"Don't start trying to pacify me," Ealasaid said sharply, drawing her hand away angrily. "I'm trying to tell you the story dispassionately because I want your advice. If you're not going to listen or believe me, I might as well . . ." She stood up and went over to the window.

"Wait a bit," I protested. "I'm not trying to pacify anyone. I'm simply trying to get you to put things into perspective. It's a bit sudden to suggest that Torrance has been murdered. Things don't normally happen that way."

"Normally. Exactly. That's what I'm trying to say. Things are all far from normal. There's this third point I mentioned to you."

"Come and sit down again. You make me nervous pacing about like that."

Reluctantly she came and sat down again, but the chair was further away from the bed now. "Well, all right. As I said, I only got back from New York yesterday morning. Both at my office and at home there was a message waiting for me from an old boy friend of mine. He's a civil servant. He said he wanted to see me urgently. Eventually he came round last night. This time it *was* a case of someone wanting me to speak to my father on his behalf. I was shocked at first. It was very unlike . . . unlike him to use anyone. He . . . He's an earnest, independent sort of person. He started at me straightaway, very wildly, about neo-colonialism, foreign economic domination, all that sort of thing. He said he'd read a piece of in-depth research on the range and extent of foreign ownership of industries and firms in this country, and what he had discovered was the enormous extent to which this has already happened, so much so that nearly all our basic industries and our technologically advanced companies too, are now foreign-owned."

The coincidence was odd and I interrupted her. "Of course in any democracy, this sort of thing is carefully watched. There are lots of controls, by Ministries, by Banks and so on. It can't go too far without being spotted." I smiled reassuringly.

"But . . . my friend . . . has discovered that many of the groups and companies have gone to extreme lengths to disguise this financial control, aided and abetted by some of these democratic watchdogs you've just mentioned." Ealasaid paused dramatically. "As I said, he's not the hysterical type, so I asked him why he had come to me. He should surely make his suspicions known in his own Ministry. He said he had done just that, but he was slapped down. You see he's heard from a number of sources that some of the work has been suppressed, at what level he isn't quite sure. The long and short of it is that the research paper that has gone forward is totally distorted. He wanted to tell my father all about it, wanted me to arrange for him to call on him secretly. He believes there's a conspiracy to . . ."

"Have you put him on to your father?" I was beginning to grasp things.

"Not yet. Father's not the easiest person for a junior civil servant like my friend to approach. He's a strict believer in the formal channels of communication. It would go very much against him from the outset, even if . . . er . . . Father doesn't much care for him either you see, ever since he caught him outside my window late one night."

"Quite right too," I smiled. "So you come to me instead. But what can I do? I'm about to go out of circulation for three weeks."

"Well he tells me you were the Minister who asked for the report in the first place."

"That's right. I have the paper here. It seems all right to me." I reacted easily. I'm not quite sure why I wasn't quite open with her about my own immediate worries about the report. Perhaps I wanted to hear her side of the story before revealing mine. In any case I was cautious. It was one thing for a junior official to go talking about such things; for a Minister to do so was a much more significant event, even if he were talking in private and to a friend.

"Will you see him?" she asked. "On a personal basis?"

I suddenly had an insight into what and whom she was talking about. "Guthrie is my Private Secretary. He can speak to me any time," I said sharply.

She gasped. "How did you know it was him?"

"I'm not in a geriatric ward yet." I was more than a trifle irritated now that I had her confirmation that it was indeed Guthrie. He had had no right to talk to her about such confidential matters.

She realised I was angry. "Oh, please," she said. "He doesn't know I've asked you. He'd be very upset."

"I'm sure he would."

She looked as if she were about to cry. "He said you'd be the only person, but he couldn't bring himself to approach you. It wasn't part of his job as your Private Secretary to go running to you with his suspicions, and in any case, his relationship with you, he said, was . . . coldly formal." Remembering that Guthrie had tried to tell me something just over an hour previously, I said nothing. I began looking for some method of saying that I felt it was entirely the wrong way to go about things, yet of saying it without hurting her. Thankfully the Sister came in then and announced that my doctor was about to come to do some clinical tests. Ealasaid would have to leave. She mustn't be here when he arrived.

Ealasaid started pleading with me to give her an answer. I felt I was letting her down, but I told her, as patiently and as pleasantly as I could, that it was impossible; I was just about to be operated on. She came to her senses at that and apologised for her thoughtlessness. She asked me not to hold it against Guthrie. I told her not to worry, but inside me I was not so sure that I wouldn't. He should not have . . . or was it jealousy? At that latter thought, I added a fraction guiltily, that I'd contact her as soon as I was able to have visitors again.

"I hope you will," she said sadly. "Meanwhile what am I to do about the job and about . . . ?"

"Guthrie can wait," I replied. "And I'd take the Bondi job if I were you." I really meant it, but as Ealasaid pushed out of the room and the doctor appeared, I realised, once again, that we had hardly parted in the best of ways.

TWELVE

IT WAS LIKE any other week-day morning. Sir Alexander
MacDowall, Secretary to the Cabinet, left home at precisely
nine o'clock in his chauffeur-driven Rover. His large Victorian
house, set well back from the road behind high granite walls
six miles to the south of Edinburgh, was left empty. He kept
no help, his daughter was already at her new desk in her City
office and his wife was in Inverness staying with a widowed
sister for a long weekend.

A methodical man, MacDowall always sat on the right-hand
side of the rear seat of the Rover as befitted his rank. His briefcase and the morning's newspapers lay beside him on the left.
When he was on official business and had a secretary with him,
he or she always knew to sit in the front, beside the driver, to
give him maximum room. But, as always in the mornings, he
was alone. The only difference on that particular day was that,
as he left the house, he realised he had left a book he had been
reading in his bedroom and went back to get it, handing his
briefcase and papers to his chauffeur as he did so. It was a
perfectly straightforward thing to do. The book, a new biography of Disraeli, he had been reading far into the night, and
while he knew that the day in front of him was a busy one, he
promised himself at least half an hour's relaxation with it,
along with a sandwich lunch at his desk.

When he came down to the car again he noted with a flicker
of annoyance that his chauffeur, in a fit of absentmindedness,
had thoughtlessly placed his briefcase and papers on the right
hand of the rear seat. He thought about telling the man to move
them, or to push them across himself, but he decided not to fuss.
It was a beautiful morning. He was getting too pernickety, and
besides, what did it matter? He climbed into the Rover and
settled down on the left-hand seat.

The car turned down the short drive, along a side road and then pulled north on to the approach road to the M1 Motorway, a gleaming new dual-carriageway that allowed him to get to the Cabinet Office, traffic permitting, within an easy half-hour. MacDowall disliked speed, preferring to leave that little bit earlier, preferring also to be able to glance his way through the morning papers with minimum discomfort. Though there was plenty of power under the bonnet, the chauffeur drove with restraint. He knew about sticking to the inside lane most of the way, only overtaking the occasional heavy lorry when absolutely necessary.

A tall, uninspired block of council flats, perhaps fifteen storeys high and five years old, now sited far too close for comfort to the bend in the new motorway. A high stone wall had been built between the two which cut off none of the traffic noise for the tenants, but it did act as a barrier preventing anyone from getting from the flats to the motorway or vice versa. The concrete facings on the building itself were badly stained, and the whole structure had already taken on a squalid and careworn aspect. It was an often-repeated example of one of the badly-sited, high-rise superslums which the architectural profession had bequeathed to the nation in a regrettably prolonged period of collective insanity. Curtainless windows on the second floor indicated an empty council flat. The previous tenants had dramatically won the pools and now lived uneasily in an ugly red-roofed house in Morningside.

The big man in the anorak, canvas bag containing his plumber's tools, had been working in the empty flat since just after eight o'clock. The peroxide woman in the flat across the stairhead nagged her husband about it with the bitter remark that council workmen never came early on the occasions when they had anything go wrong with the pipes.

Once inside the flat, the man in the anorak stopped worrying about how they had arranged for the key to be available. That some minor official at the town hall had been bribed was none of his affair. They had assured him that he wouldn't be disturbed; nevertheless he locked and bolted the door behind him.

He went straight through to the empty kitchen and looked expertly out of the window down on to the motorway. It either had to be from the kitchen or from the lavatory, and after a quick inspection he opted for the former; there was more elbow room. He bent down, opened his canvas bag and took out the little transistor radio. He switched it on; there was a slight mush at first, but it was pre-set. He waited a moment or so, then the radio emitted seven careful bleeps. It would repeat this every two minutes, precisely. They wouldn't be noticed on the air. Speech, though preferable, was out on security grounds.

The man returned to his bag and took out a tripod, extending the legs so that the top came just above the level of the window. He glanced at his watch. There was still a clear half-hour to go, allowing for the target being a bit early. He pulled the gun out from its case and fitted it on to the tripod. Then, clipping on the peculiarly-shaped silencer, he bent over and, aiming at a carefully-chosen spot on the tarmac on the far lane of the motorway, adjusted the telescopic sights. The range was rather great for perfection, but he was no amateur; the gun was also a professional. He did a few dry runs on unsuspecting private cars, judging their speed and position on the motorway, lightly pressing the trigger at the precise moment when their drivers hit the centre of the cross in the telescope lens. At the end of ten minutes, had the gun been loaded, he was sure he would have scored at least nine out of ten. It was going to be easy; an excellent vantage point, with no other buildings overlooking the windows of the flat.

It would be child's play even without the assistance he saw coming along the motorway. Five minutes to nine, and a red and yellow striped lorry, amber light flashing on the roof of its cab, drove up and stopped a little short of the block of flats. Two men got out and rapidly started putting up "Road

Works" signs and distributing luminescent red and white plastic cones, narrowing the three-lane motorway down to one. All traffic would have to slow down.

The man in the anorak looked at his watch again. It was a minute or two after planned arrival time. He hoped nothing had gone wrong. Every two minutes the radio had continued emitting its seven bleeps. The man took a can of Coca Cola from the bag, pulled the tag which opened it, and drank the lot with hardly a breath. As he finished, the radio started producing urgent and continuous bleeps. The car had passed the bridge a mile back up the motorway. The man put the empty can down slowly, without an obvious care in the world, and positioned himself easily behind the gun.

The chauffeur slowed down appreciably when he saw the first of the signs announcing single lane traffic ahead. MacDowall looked up automatically from his *Scotsman*, noted the road signs and the long neat row of warning cones, glanced at his watch and frowned slightly. He was already a few minutes late. Each morning, he subconsciously noted the time as he passed the big ugly block of flats on the right of the motorway. It was exactly fifteen safe driving minutes from his office. If there were road works ahead as well, he really would be late. He was aware of his incipient fussiness. What was five minutes more or less to a man in his position? Only the other day he had heard one of the security guards say, with an empty imprecation, that they could all set their watches by the promptness of his arrival time. Was that such a quality?

Four or five bullets smacked into the roof of the car, a stray one smashing through the side window. Several of them neatly punctured the leather of the right-hand rear seat, two via precise round holes in MacDowall's briefcase and discarded newspapers. One further chance bullet, perhaps deflected by the angle of the roof, found its true target and embedded itself solidly in his shoulder. Another ricocheted wildly through the glossy cover of the biography of Disraeli. Despite the shock, his good left hand automatically held on to the shredded book.

It was the chauffeur, Tank Corps trained in his youth to little normal benefit, who cottoned on to what was happening with remarkable perception, and accelerated rapidly away, knocking down the line of plastic warning cones in the process. A rear tyre had been burst, but that was a nicety, and the chauffeur pulled to a stop on a verge only when they were safely under the shelter of a bridge, over the motorway. MacDowall, slouched in the back, ashen-faced but conscious, kept trying to turn to identify where the shots had come from. "The big block back there, Sir, second or third floor, judging from the angle. You all right, Sir . . . ?" The man dried up, then he saw the blood. Leaving MacDowall where he was, he jumped rapidly from the car, ran to the roadside and started trying to wave down the passing cars. Remarkably for the time of day, no other cars had been in the vicinity when the attack had happened, and there were no apparent witnesses to anything being amiss.

Two or three cars and a lorry thundered imperviously past, presuming, uncharitably, to avoid the mere bother of helping a man with a puncture. Then a routine police car patrol, on urgent watch for speeding motorists, was on the scene, and the chauffeur was pouring out his story. Some valuable moments were lost before the officers, at last provoked by the choice of language with which the chauffeur eventually described their stupidity, got out of the warmth of their car to go over and inspect the Rover. To do them credit, the speed of their subsequent activities left little to be desired, but the assassin's vantage point had been well chosen, the high barrier wall lining the motorway was impossible to negotiate at speed from where they were, and by the time other squad cars, summoned by radio, got to the building and located the empty flat, it really was empty. There wasn't even a fingerprinted Coca Cola tin left behind. A well-planned operation, except for the chance seating arrangement which caused its failure. And when they got the Secretary to the Cabinet to the Casualty Department of the hospital some ten minutes later, he was still fiercely clutching the remains of the Disraeli biography in his good left hand.

It was about an hour later. The bare little room buried deep in the Special Task Unit's nondescript office block close by Leith docks, was cold despite the two-bar heater set into the wall. The unsurfaced breeze-block walls imparted their own chill to the atmosphere. There was a metal fire door and no windows. High up, near the ceiling, was a ventilator grating from which came the low hum of the air filtering system. On one wall, the only sign of decoration, someone had Sellotaped the centre pin-up from a *Playboy* magazine; July's nameless playmate, yet another sexless, bulging doll with unblemished plastic skin and immaculate hairdressing. A clock on the wall showed ten-thirty. A battered trestle table stood against one wall and on it were two or three chipped mugs filled with blackened dregs, a half-empty milk bottle, some instant coffee and scruffy paper packets of tea and sugar. The centre of the room was taken up with what one might, at first, be forgiven for mistaking as a small telephone exchange; the flexes and sockets were there, but there was also a peculiar series of dials and meters set into the equipment casing. From time to time red lights flashed urgently on and off.

In front of the apparatus, there were three tubular steel chairs, two of which were occupied. One man, middle-aged, fixedly faced his series of dials, a pair of headphones clamped over his ears. Unlike a telephone operator's, there was no mouthpiece attached to them since his job was only to listen. He had a pad of paper in front of him on which, from time to time, he jotted notes. To his right, a small side-table carried a rather efficient-looking tape recorder which the man occasionally adjusted. The other man in the room, much younger, long greasy hair, and with a very bad complexion, was sitting back in his chair thumbing through an old copy of *Playboy*, possibly the same issue that had provided the wall décor. He looked bored. There were no red lights flashing at his position as he had a very selective target.

Suddenly a warning buzzer sounded and a light flashed in front of the youth. He rapidly picked up his set of headphones and put them on. At the same time he switched on the tape recorder he too had beside him. He started taking shorthand notes.

About a mile away in a very select suburb of the city, Ian Campbell, Governor of the Reserve Bank, picked up the telephone, listened for a moment and then said, "Oh, it's you, is it? Good morning," in a drawling upper-class English accent. "Yes, I'm well, thank you."

The voice at the other end was slow and deliberate, and the young long-haired youth tapping the line had no difficulty in getting down every word that was said. So often people spoke both rapidly and indistinctly, and he had to check his notes against the tape recording before submitting his report.

"We thought you'd be interested to know that we're moving into phase two," the slow voice said. It wasn't strictly an American accent, though there was a suspicion of a transatlantic vowel sound from time to time. "We're opening the game up a bit."

"Yes?" said Ian Campbell cautiously. He was always cautious on the telephone, and was fully justified, though he would never know how much.

"We're ringing to ask for news."

"What about?" The spotty long-haired youth noted down that Campbell's voice betrayed anxiety. His readers liked the background.

"A hunt . . . A shoot. Have you heard what the bag was?"

"Oh my God . . ." There was silence for a moment.

"Are you still there?"

"Yes . . . That . . . that was you, was it?"

"Yes." There was a long pause. The spotty youth tapped his pencil on his pad impatiently.

"Not up to your usual standards of expertise, then," said Campbell eventually, composure apparently regained.

"He missed?"

"More or less. Back at his desk with his arm in a sling by mid-day at the latest, that's what they're saying. But why the hell him? And why so vicious? There are other ways of persuasion."

"Not everyone has your superb lack of principle," the trans-atlantic-tinged voice responded evenly. There was a pause. "But you're right. It *was* careless. We'll see if it's shaken him. Perhaps he'll be more amenable to inducements now. Honour often goes when fear plays master."

"I doubt it; not with him."

"So do I, but we'll try. Rather, you'll try."

"No I won't," said Ian Campbell nervously.

"Yes, dammit, you will." The voice was suddenly sharp. "You make an appointment to see him today. Report back tonight, Mr Governor." The title was thrown out with no veil on the sarcasm.

"I . . . I . . ."

The spotty youth noted the precise time the line went dead. He noted also the invective uttered by the Governor of the Reserve Bank into the dead receiver. The youth left the bare cold room, asking his colleague to keep watch on his lines as he went. There was an elderly typewriter in the next room; he'd better get the intercept off without delay. As he hadn't heard about the assassination attempt, he couldn't make full sense of the conversation. But he wasn't as stupid as first impression might have indicated, and he knew that Governors of Reserve Banks were not usually addressed in such forthright terms. He sat down in front of the machine, slipped the ribbon key down and began by typing the word *Immediate* in prominent red capitals.

Sir Alexander MacDowall was a most able man. He would not otherwise have reached and remained where he was. He was no part of the order of things whereby men so often are promoted one rank too far, to what has been called their level of incompetence. Had there been higher ranks in his life, this particular Secretary to the Cabinet would have climbed them.

Perhaps his most outstanding quality was in assessing and judging his fellow men. It has long been a part of his official life, advising and selecting the right individual for the right appointment. It had been his regret that with this power and ability to judge, he had never had the opportunity to select those political figures for whom he nominally worked. With candour, and no glimpse of modesty, he realised how much better the Government of the country would have been had he, and not the Prime Minister, selected and appointed the present Cabinet. Most outside appointments in the gift of the State and all senior ones in the Civil Service, were his selection or had his blessing. There was only one major one where he had, he admitted, slipped up drastically, and that was over the appointment of the Governor of the Reserve Bank. To his mind, Mr Ian Campbell was an unmitigated disaster. But he had assumed, until that day at least, that the tragic nature of the appointment lay in the poor, weak quality of the incumbent. Campbell, undistinguished in every field, had, at first, been totally lost in the international monetary world, since his merchant-banking background, of a limited bond-trading nature, added to the aristocratic decadence of his background, had hardly suited him for his now powerful role. Later, he had moved to the more dangerous stage, all too common with politicians, of coupling incompetence with a certain frenetic activity. Latterly, there were more devious factors at work as well.

MacDowall, in considerable pain from the flesh wound in his shoulder, was at his desk trying, bravely, or stubbornly, to catch up on his work. Released from a reluctant hospital at mid-day, despite protests from the doctors, he was back in his office as if nothing had happened. He had just emerged from a brief and inconclusive meeting with the Prime Minister who had anxiously congratulated him on his escape. The Prime Minister, charitable enough, had seemed characteristically unconcerned at the real significance of the attack, and even for him, was hardly up to the occasion, his senility showing through more than usual.

That interview over, MacDowall had had to cope with a flood of well-wishers and other anxious enquirers, as the news of the assassination attempt got round. He drafted an anodyne unsensational press release for the papers, in an attempt to take a little of the heat out of the occasion. It wouldn't satisfy them long, as well he knew. His wife had rung frantically from Inverness, insisting on returning at once; his daughter, Ealasaid, arrived to make sure he was all right; the Commissioner of Police was on the line at half-hour intervals with nil progress reports about the hunt for the gunman; he was beginning, for once, to feel more than a little strained.

To top it all, his personal assistant came in with the news that Campbell wanted to see him at once. In other circumstances he would have arranged for her to say that he was too busy. But he had, for one thing, just read the text of the telephone intercept, brought to him urgently in an envelope covered with red seals, and for another, the door opened as his PA was talking, and Campbell came in unasked; this despite the protestation of the uniformed policeman who was now stationed outside the door. Campbell's face was white and drawn, imparting, so MacDowall thought, a momentary tinge of interest to a normally tedious man.

Campbell began by gushing out empty congratulations at MacDowall's good fortune. There was a lengthy pause. Eventually, MacDowall looked up from his desk enquiringly.

"You wanted something, Governor?"

"Yes, that is, I came to . . . warn you." Again there was a pause.

"About what may I ask? It's a little late, for example, to warn me about being attacked." MacDowall stared hard at Campbell over his rimless glasses.

"They were trying to kill you."

"I presume so."

"You must be more forthcoming with them, more reasonable. You owe it to yourself, your family, to the country."

"What are you talking about?"

"You know. I know that they . . . that people have been trying to persuade you . . ."

". . . to give them a free hand to do what they want: to take over the country. Is that what you're talking about?"

"We'll go under as a nation. We're done for politically and economically, without their help. I should know."

"You should indeed, Governor. You should indeed. Did they send you? Did they? Are they your friends, Governor? Are they? You chose dangerous bed-fellows if they are. It's I who should perhaps be warning you. Or is it too late?" The Secretary to the Cabinet stood up. He felt an unaccustomed anger inside him. For him it was a most uncharacteristic outburst.

"I'm trying to help," said Campbell weakly. He was shaken by MacDowall's unexpected vehemence. For a moment MacDowall wondered if the other man was going to break down.

"They're going to be in touch with you again, Secretary. Please be reasonable. It's . . . think of it as a business deal. Other people, more . . . more senior than you are . . . are being amenable. You're standing in their way. They know you're too powerful, so . . . so if you won't co-operate, I'm sure they'll try again."

"I don't need you to teach me what to do, Mr Governor," MacDowall said, his voice now controlled and like ice. "I don't wish to discuss the matter further with you."

"I've to tell them you refuse to co-operate?" Campbell asked.

"There's still something called morality." MacDowall spoke slowly and deliberately. "Now, please will you *leave*."

The Governor of the Reserve Bank started to say something more but then caught sight of the hard, cold face. MacDowall had turned away to stare unseeingly out of the window over the city's grey roofs. Campbell hesitated for a moment then turned and falteringly left the room.

As soon as he had gone, MacDowall collapsed back in his chair. He wiped the back of his good hand across his forehead. He was getting old, he had lost a lot of blood that morning, and he knew all too well that he should still be in bed. But appearances were important and he had to think. Things, things about which he had long known and suspected, odd offers of patronage, of money, never direct, never open, never attributable, were recalled one by one. He had had in front of him for long enough a picture of widening corruption and yet he had failed to act. It had been another error of judgment on his part. Now it was almost too late. He had to presume that Campbell meant what he said, that the Government had been infiltrated far and deeply. If this was indeed the case, who could be trusted? He had to presume that many famous names, many of his immediate colleagues at the top, had already been won over. He had long suspected as much, but had deluded himself until now. A Mafia, a freemasonry of perjured men. He had been aware through intelligence reports, through the evidence of his own eyes, of people being picked off, one by one. Not everyone was approached; just the more influential, the more important, the weaker ones perhaps. By such methods the strong became isolated and alone.

It was pointless, he realised, getting upset and angry at people like Governor Campbell. Campbell was a weak front man, probably one of the first to be corrupted. It was those behind him . . .

MacDowall picked up the transcript of Campbell's telephone call. It had taken enormous reserves of self-control to speak even in as civilised a way as he had just done to a man who was in such obviously close touch with the people, whoever they were, who had ordered the attempt on his life. By having the transcript, it meant that he was one step ahead; better informed. But in the end, it hadn't helped him resolve the enormous problem that faced him.

For an instant, as the pain in his shoulder rose in intensity, he felt like packing it in. He was only a civil servant after all. If the politicians wanted it that way, who was he to stand in their way? He could resign. He could simply stand aside and not continue to act as a lone barrier against the financial and political forces that were seeking to control the country. But the mood passed. It might not be too late. He couldn't cope alone. He needed others. Where were the strong, uncorrupted men? He must find them out. He needed allies, people he could trust.

On an impulse he picked up his telephone receiver. "When does the Minister of Home Affairs get out of hospital?" he asked his PA sharply.

Ian Campbell, a broken reed for the moment, was reporting his failure by telephone. When he had finished, his interrogator said abruptly:

"Then we move to the next stage. You know what we want you to do. Don't worry. We'll be behind you the whole time. We'll give you precise instructions. And I'm sure you've always wanted the job."

"I . . . I . . . yes . . ." Campbell muttered.

"I'm so glad," said the interrogator. "It would have caused us minor difficulties otherwise."

"But no more shooting. No more bombings."

"Why, I'll grant you that, Campbell. Tomorrow there'll be no need any more, so long as everyone behaves and obeys the laws of this land of yours."

THIRTEEN

I WAS RELEASED from hospital at 9.30 in the morning. Ingram and a man called Dobbs from the Ministry, who had occasionally stood in for Guthrie when the latter was on leave, were waiting at the main door, as was a lone press photographer and a bearded TV newsreel cameraman who took a few uninspired shots of me shaking hands with the hospital matron and senior registrar.

I was still in my wheelchair. Apart from my doctors and the muscular lady physiotherapist, no one outside the hospital knew that the operation had proved surprisingly effective, that I had gained a little power back in my leg muscles. And there was still such a thing as professional medical confidence, so no one need get to know. It was early days, the possibility of my actually ever being able to walk unaided was still remote, the pain was intense, and I just didn't want everyone to know what was going on. It was my own private problem and gossip about a supposed recovery and the effusions from press and public that would follow such a revelation, I wanted to avoid at all cost.

Part of the price I had paid for this partial success was a distinctly longer stay in hospital than I had anticipated. It was four weeks to the day, and during that time, try as I might, I had not been allowed to keep up fully with my work. I saw hardly any official papers; my Private Secretary Guthrie was, I was told, on holiday taking advantage of my absence, though I imagined that he might be just keeping out of my way, and even a lot of my personal and constituency mail, though it passed through my hands, was dealt with on a caretaker basis by my office. I fretted of course, but it is difficult to be forceful in submissively clinical surroundings, and my occasional visitors—such as the Secretary to the Cabinet—all in obvious conspiracy with and vetted by my doctors, kept pacifying me, urging that my health came first. I never heard once from my wife. It didn't much worry me, but we had been married for a long time, and time is no idle factor even in bad relationships. Nor did I hear from Ealasaid, and that did worry me.

I felt rather dream-like and out of touch as I was driven away from the hospital that morning. I was keen to get back to my desk and papers, but I was so much in ignorance that I didn't even know what, if any, official programme of duties had been arranged for me. In desultory fashion, Dobbs began briefing me on minor matters through the glass window of the driving compartment. He was a morose, podgy man at the best of times, but today I felt he was more than usually unforthcoming. However, I put it down to my mood rather than his. He talked vaguely about briefing meetings, getting up to date and so on without actually going into things in any detail. I asked irritably where Guthrie was. Surely he wasn't still on holiday? A fraction oddly, Dobbs told me that his leave had been extended, that I'd hear later on. Then I asked about the news report of the assassination attempt on the Secretary to the Cabinet, but even on this Dobbs was remarkably taciturn. It crossed my mind that I should suggest to Personnel that they find me a livelier, if less efficient, stand-in for Guthrie in the future.

I decided to leave further discussion till we reached the office. I slid the glass window between myself and the driving compartment shut, and surreptitiously eased my legs, first one and then the other, to prove to myself that their new-found movement wasn't in some mysterious way confined to the hospital. The legs jerked slowly and painfully back to life and, having proved this much to myself, I settled back with a certain degree of satisfaction. Gazing absentmindedly from the window, I wondered a little at the route Ingram had chosen to drive from the hospital, which was right on the outskirts, to the office situated in the city centre. It was raining now and the blackened houses and factories of the industrial area through which we were passing, seemed all the more desolate and grim. How pleasant it was nevertheless to be back in harness again. I felt almost happy, additionally so with the perverse satisfaction of my aching legs.

A white roadsign at a crossroad, and Ingram turned left rather than right, definitely away from the city. I jerked myself into partial alertness. I had a job to do. What was going on? Had I misunderstood Dobbs? I leaned forward and pushed back the glass partition.

"Where are we going, Dobbs? I understood we were going straight to the Ministry," I enquired briskly. To my surprise there was no response whatsoever and I thought at first he hadn't heard me. Raising my voice, I repeated the question. Again Dobbs ignored me. I felt I was dreaming. Had the man gone deaf, or was he asleep?

I spoke sharply to Ingram.

"Where are we going, Ingram?"

Ingram's attention moved momentarily from the road and glancing nervously at Dobbs he broke out: "Sorry, Minister. Orders is orders. . . . Sorry," he repeated. To my amazement Dobbs reacted vehemently to this totally mysterious statement, turned on Ingram and sharply told him to shut up and stick to his driving.

"What the bloody hell are you on about, Dobbs?" I leaned forward again and bellowed. "Have you taken leave of your senses?" As I did so, I banged my hand frustratedly against the half-open glass partition.

Dobbs turned in his seat, and screwing up his little mongoloid face said in an infuriatingly insolent yet precise tone, "It will do little good getting angry, Mr Mockingham. Times have changed . . . from today. I advise you to sit quietly. Things will be explained to you in due course. You're a sick man, after all."

I exploded at that. "I don't care what your explanations are, Dobbs. I've had quite enough. Consider yourself dismissed as

from now. Ingram, turn round and drive straight to the Ministry. With no further trouble if you please."

As I had somehow already anticipated, my outburst had no
effect whatsoever, and my order was totally ignored. Perhaps
it was the fact that Dobbs had addressed me as *Mr Mockingham*
and not as *Minister* that had served to warn me. I felt as if I
were experiencing one of those fantasy dreams where one finds
oneself powerless to prevent some event and so one wakes up
to escape it. I recalled, at the same time, a real occasion when I
was a National Service lieutenant in charge of a platoon on
patrol in Korea just towards the end of the fighting. I had a
fairly rebellious soldier in the platoon with whom I had long
had trouble, and I came across him one morning lying asleep
at his sentry post. I had bellowed at him. He hadn't responded.
I had a moment of mental panic at my authority being so
totally flouted. A glimpse of potential headlines about mutiny
flashed across my mind until I realised that the man wasn't
rebelling. He was dead. We never found the sniper, though he
picked off my Sergeant as well when we started carrying the
man's body back to base.

I sat back in the car seat, gripping the leather arm-rest for
mental more than physical support and tried to figure out what
was happening. The sweat slid unpleasantly between my palms
and the hide. Had it been Dobbs alone, I would have put it
down to a brainstorm or something similar. But Ingram, a
totally sane man if there was one, was in it as well. He at least
was patently unhappy at what he was having to do. But he
was doing it, disobeying me for some reason, without any real
effort to defy Dobbs.

For a few moments I remained numbed and silent. Then in
what I hoped sounded an utterly composed voice, I quietly
asked what was going on. "Where are you taking me? Am I
being kidnapped or something?" I dried up as once again
there was no response. I felt that to continue in this vein
would have led to the indignity of my losing all self-control,
especially as it had now become clear that kidnapping was the

only word I could dream up to describe what was happening
to me.

I remembered reading the experiences of some diplomat
kidnapped by rebels somewhere in South America. He had
described the suspension of disbelief he had experienced, and
had continued to experience until he saw a policeman being
gunned down in the brown dusty street in an attempt to stop
his kidnappers' car. Thereafter, the diplomat's mind had con-
centrated itself wonderfully. Perhaps I should count myself
lucky not to have some similar incident with which to focus
my conscious mind.

I tried to relax, to think out a meaning for it all. It was too
much to take after the weeks of peace and tranquillity in the
hospital. But there was little to be gained by speculating. For a
moment I thought of trying to exert my will by force, using up
the slight, new-found power in my legs as ally. But some part
of my subconscious held me back. I might need that trifling
element of effort later.

What did one do? Again I remembered the diplomat. He
had tried to memorise where he was being taken. But I had
little need to do that now, for I had just driven into my own
parliamentary constituency, where I prided myself on knowing
nearly every road and turning. Ten minutes passed. We were
out in the open countryside now. I recognised many of the
individual farms and cottages as we passed. I switched back to
Dobbs. Why should he be acting as he now was? What did
he have against me? We had always got on reasonably well
when he had worked for me, if never closely or warmly. He
seemed a practical if dull civil servant. He should have no
grudges. Not against politicians at least. To civil servants,
people like myself were additional factors to be taken into
account in the general decision-making process. A bad or
difficult Minister was like an act of God or a natural disaster.
Civil Servants didn't grudge such things; they planned to
circumvent them peacefully. And that should have gone for
Ingram too, only more so. Unless, unbeknown to me, my wife

had eventually got round to dismissing his wife, our cook/ housekeeper. But that was hardly likely either as fact or motive. I found myself staring hard at the back of Dobbs's neck. Hard thick, black closely-cropped hair. There was a scar in the thick flesh just at the bottom of the hairline. The mark of an adolescent boil rather than a wound. He had bad dandruff.

I looked round curiously as we turned sharply off the main road by a double-gated house. It was strange. I used to know this big house so well. It had, for centuries, belonged to the same noble family. Then, like so many, both family and house had run to seed. The family had scattered and the big house had been sold. I remembered that the Bondi Corporation had bought it some four years ago as an executive training school.

The heavy, intricately-wrought iron gates had been reno- vated and repainted. The old coat of arms set in the stonework of the pillars, had been retained and was now, a trifle garishly, picked out in crimson and gold. The gates themselves were closed, but Ingram sounded his horn, and a man appeared immediately from one neat, well-kept gatehouse. He was in blue battle-dress uniform with a white-brimmed peak cap of the sort that American security guards wear. By his side paced an alsatian on a short chain. The man unlocked the gates and came out to the car. Dobbs produced what looked like an identity card of a type I hadn't seen before. A passport-type photograph was embossed in one corner. The guard looked at a list he carried in his free hand and checked off a name. "You're expected," he said brusquely in an unmistakable American accent. Then he saluted, turned away to open the gates wide, and Ingram drove on through and up the long drive. The gates were closed at once behind us. I had a momen- tary glimpse of a new high perimeter fence, running to left and right away from the gate. It was so efficient-looking that I was surprised I hadn't noticed it before from the outside, since I passed that way fairly often. But then I realised it had been set back a bit from the original old wall of the estate, discreetly out of sight among the trees.

The drive itself and the lawns on each side were in beautiful order, so unlike the wilderness of neglect when I had last been there some five years before. As we swept up the gravel to the house, I noticed at least two gardeners working among the rose beds, spring pruning and hoeing. The big house itself had taken on its old elegance once again, or perhaps more so, since I doubted it had ever looked so immaculate. There were two or three expensive-looking cars parked outside, a Rolls-Royce, at least two enormous American cars, and one or two official Rovers like my own.

Ingram pulled to a halt at the bottom of the steps. Our journey was obviously over. Dobbs and he got out and started unloading my wheelchair as if nothing unusual had happened. I made no move, briefly deciding to be stubborn. But before I committed myself to this course of action, Dobbs opened the car door and addressed me sharply:

"I would co-operate fully if I were you, Mr Mockingham. Everything will be explained now, to your enlightment if not to your satisfaction. It would be unseemly if we had to carry you in any more helpless than usual." He stood back unconcerned and aloof, and I decided both to retain my vestiges of dignity and do as he said. I could only presume that he meant it when he used the quaint old-fashioned word *unseemly*.

Out and into my wheelchair; then Ingram and Dobbs carried me, as usual, backwards up the long steps to the main door. I was facing away from the house as it is easier to manipulate a wheelchair that way, so it was only when we got to the top that I appreciated the welcoming party.

There were two of them: Carlyle and de Laski. The brash New York businessman and the little dark Maltese Glaswegian with his Sherlock Holmes pipe, those two rather odd members of the Federation Executive whom I had last seen well over a month and a half ago in New York.

"Good morning, Mr Mockingham. Glad to see you out of

hospital. You've been out of circulation for quite a few weeks."

Preposterously, Carlyle was smiling at me as if nothing was out of order. The *Mr Mockingham* bit jarred once again.

"Would you, if you know, mind telling me precisely what is going on? Dobbs here, who's standing in for Guthrie my Private Sectretary, seems to have gone off his head," I blustered.

"We know Mr Dobbs well. He has had a difficult job to do. We felt Mr Guthrie might not be the best person for the task," responded Carlyle as if that explained everything. "I . . . we are sorry if you feel yourself in some way inconvenienced. Come inside and I'll see if we can fix up a cup of the hideous concoction that passes for coffee in this country. Mr Dobbs, we *must* do something about the catering." I started to say something, to ask about Guthrie, but Carlyle turned and walked away into the hallway, and I was pushed after him. I held back my renewed fury with my surprise. If only I could play my totally cold reputation from now on.

The beautiful entrance hall was also as I remembered it. The ceiling, ornate and gilded, had been recently well restored, and the stags' heads and suits of armour, bought up with the house, still adorned the walls in ostentatious profusion. The only new additions were a reception desk, behind which was sitting quite a pretty girl, and behind her in an alcove that had once held a marble statue, a large metal control panel with many flashing lights set into it: the indicator board for an extensive burglar alarm system. The girl smiled at me as I passed.

I was wheeled, unprotesting, through the hall and into what was still the library. It too was considerably changed, neater, cleaner, and there were several new, tastefully modern chairs and tables scattered about the room to replace the old shabby furniture that I remembered. I was wheeled up to a large conference-type table in the centre. Carlyle and de Laski seated themselves opposite me, rather like an interview board. Dobbs and Ingram, having thus positioned me, left the room, closing the door behind them.

"Coffee?" asked Carlyle at once, pushing a silver tray with cup and coffee pot towards me. I ignored it coldly.

"Very well," said Carlyle briskly. "I agree we owe you an explanation first. Civilities, I hope, will come afterwards. De Laski will explain." He sat back in his chair and folded his arms. I stared back at him uncomprehendingly. My legs had started to ache uncontrollably, but the pain helped in a strange way to sharpen my senses.

"It's not a *coup d'état*," de Laski began quietly. "That sounds much too dramatic. Think of it more as a take-over bid."

I must have made some gesture of disbelief, for de Laski and Carlyle turned to each other and smiled slightly, in the patronising sort of way one might adopt towards a child who had said something funny or foolish.

"To begin at the beginning would be unnecessary, I think," he went on after a moment. "You must have been aware, in your position, even before you went into hospital, that something like this was going on. We believe you'd even gotten to the length of asking for a report. But to put it in a nutshell for you, the situation now is that we have, one way or another, already acquired the majority holding in almost all of your major, and very many of your minor, industries."

I listened to the words, fascinated by de Laski's accent. It was hard to pinpoint: an odd mixture of American, Mediterranean and Scottish; vowels mixed and distorted in unexpected but not unpleasant ways. It was frequently blurred by his habit of keeping his pipe in his mouth as he spoke. Then I began to concentrate on the meaning, remembering again the report I had read from Matthews in the Department of Trade and Industrial Development just before my operation. I remembered something Ealasaid MacDowall had told me at the same time, about Guthrie's worries. Where was he now?

"Then, by diligent preparation, we have succeeded in acquiring almost the entire country's news media." De Laski was still talking.

"You were behind the bombing of the transmitters?" I

blurted out. De Laski made a brief gesture of assent as if my question were irrelevant. "Who are you?" I went on. I was aware that my voice was hardly raised above a whisper.

"The Bondi Corporation are, as you are probably aware, a very large, American-based company, in whose Scottish Headquarters you now are. While some other subsidiary companies have been and are much concerned in this exercise, it is precise enough for your information to say that the Bondi Corporation . . ."

"You stepped in to offer help when the transmitters were blown up." The remark was self-obvious as soon as I had uttered it, but I was totally stunned by the enormity of what I was being told.

"Right first time, Mr Mockingham. So now, to put it nice and slowly for you: we had the economy, we had the news media, and we acquired a sweeping majority on the Federation Executive, incidentally, abandoning Messrs MacPake and Lindsay since we last met. All we still required was . . . the Government. And by and large we've got that too now, you and one or two others permitting."

"You mean, you're telling me . . . you're attempting to take over the whole country?" I suddenly had to restrain an urge to start laughing, but the feeling passed quickly. I clearly remembered MacPake and Torrance, those early suspicions, ridiculous at the time.

"Do have some coffee now, Mr Mockingham," Carlyle broke in. "You look rather strained. Would you like something a little stronger, or is it too early in the day?" Unthinkingly I did as was suggested and poured myself some black coffee, but I never got round to drinking it. "It's unbelievable," I said after a moment. "It's like some gigantic Mafia plot."

"This isn't confederate crime. We aren't the Mafia."

"The distinction is hard to pinpoint," I responded.

"That's unkind, Mr Mockingham. The multi-national company has been doing this sort of thing for years."

"But generally in the developing world, hand in glove with

the CIA as like as not. It was part of your post-war scramble for Africa, Asia, you name it. But till now, the Americans didn't poach on their friends."

"We aren't the US Government, nor the CIA. I don't think they'd approve. We're just a big, big company buying up assets and support as we have always done. In case you think it's an impossibility, let me read you a piece from the week's *Economist*. It says, and I quote: *The annual sales of General Motors are now bigger than the net National Incomes of all but a dozen countries in the world.* Quite a statistic, you'll agree, Mr Mockingham. Now we in the Bondi Corporation are not quite that big, but we've gone a long way towards it."

"And Scotland is the latest asset. It's bigger than you've gone for before surely." I was now genuinely curious.

"We got big by thinking big," Carlyle broke in proudly.

"There's a Dale Carnegie cliché there somewhere," I sniped.

"It's a self-evident truth," de Laski went on. "Look, Mr Mockingham, I'm putting my cards on the table. We like you. We . . . I like Scotland and the Scots. I don't want, the Corporation doesn't want, to hurt you more than you have been already. You're going to *benefit* from it, yes, you and Scotland are going to benefit."

"You're just doing us a favour? How very nice of you. And it's just out of the kindness of your corporate heart, I suppose?"

"Of course we'll benefit too," de Laski said glibly. "It's been rather tricky for us in America since you joined the European Common Market and this will give us ex-officio membership so to speak."

"That won't quite do," I responded. "A company as profit-conscious as the Bondi Corporation obviously is, has to have pretty concrete reasons for taking over a country as bankrupt and politically unstable as Scotland is."

"I could give you a lecture about our motivations, Mr Mockingham," de Laski said slowly. "I've done it often back home. But right now I just haven't the time. In any case you're intelligent enough to see many of the reasons. Why, for one thing, should we bother about tin-pot principalities as tax havens, when we can have a fully-fledged state for the asking? Scotland's going to be a very handy launching pad for a lot of our international financial and business deals in the very near future. And if we overstep the mark anytime, infringe the rules so to speak, why then we don't need to worry about the Government getting all upset by our misbehaving. We can just tear up the rule book. We see Scotland as a sort of Switzerland, without the Government restraints—or at least with only those restraints that suit us. If one were an international financier what more could one wish for? There are lots of other reasons of course; the Common Market factor I mentioned is by no means a minor one. A lot of our subsidiaries will be channelling goods into the European market from now on, without having to worry about paying Community border taxes. Scotland itself will have to pay its way of course. There may be unemployment now. Well, Mr Mockingham, there's going to be a lot more. Welfare considerations, government spending on social services and so on—such things will have to be slashed. As you said, the profit motive is our driving force, and will continue to be so even though a lot of people get hurt in the process. That's life, Mr Mockingham. But I assure you, Scotland as a whole will benefit."

"Materially, economically, I grant you it's possible that some people in Scotland could benefit—but at what price?" I hesitated. "Do you remember ever seeing a *Punch* cartoon of First World War vintage? It's famous in its way. Belgium has been overrun. The cartoon shows the King of the Belgians leaving the Ship of State. The Kaiser, a leer on his face, is leaning over the side and saying something like *See. You have lost everything*, and the King replies *Not my soul.*"

"Romantic claptrap, Mr Mockingham. Sentimental rubbish. It's not worthy of you. You're a practical man."

"You're obviously only too practical as well. I find it fascinating, if horrifying. I almost believe that we think on the same wavelength. So you must get my point. A country like

Scotland, so recently having regained its independence, isn't like another big company. It just can't be taken over."

"You want a bet, as they used to say in the movies." De Laski smiled. "But you're sure beginning to get the picture."

"You can't move in and use the same mechanisms as for a take-over," I went on. "Replace the Board of Directors, weed the middle management of its loyalists, that sort of thing."

"And precisely why not? It's a slower process admittedly. We'll not do anything drastic. The National Assembly can continue, so long as it behaves. I'm sure you'll agree that the people's representatives have seldom stopped your Administration doing what it wanted. The Assembly is a sort of safety valve producing little but rhetoric; but with people like you, we have to take more care. We convince or remove those who matter. The rest will follow."

"Why not? Because this is a democracy," I said confidently.

"Have the intelligence to smile when you use that word. Democracy is bunk."

"I'm not using it in its simplest form. But a country isn't just an organisation with two parts, employers and employees."

"Wrong again, Mr Mockingham. You're losing your intellectual detachment."

"The ordinary shares aren't for sale."

"They are indeed. So are the preference shares. That's why you're here."

FOURTEEN

THERE WERE A number of people going about their normal course of business that day whose future actions were to have an important part in the scheme of things. One of them was a man by the name of Walt Tesco, a round, myopic little man, with thick pebble glasses; a man with a decided and unattractive tendency to halitosis. Walt Tesco was a journalist by profession. Not in the main stream of his calling, but one of those semi-free-lance hacks, employed partly by an agency, which, as often as not, sent him after the less savoury items of gossip on the fringes of big names and important news stories. Tesco was adept at picking up the *human interest* items for the less respectable but more widely-read yellow magazines and newspapers of Europe and America.

Walt Tesco had been working in America for some months past, and had only very recently arrived in Edinburgh. He had been there once or twice before in his life and had a sort of love-hate relationship with that chilly grey city. He had gradually got used to it, had found a hotel he liked, and there were one or two bars in Rose Street where he felt as much at ease as he ever felt. When the Scots were drunk he found them quite approachable and easy to talk to, and in the present state of the economy there were always plenty of out-of-work journalists about who were never too bashful about accepting a drink or two from a comparative stranger.

Walt Tesco was on the track of much more than a good story this time. He was still admittedly earning part of his bread and butter in a continuing pursuit of scandal and gossip, but he had also, recently, been building up a separate dossier on something in quite a different league. It all began away back in New York after a man, who had held the post of Special Representative of the Federation of American Caledonian

Societies in Edinburgh, had been run over and killed while dead drunk. There had been one or two oddities about that case, somehow one thing had led to another, and Tesco found himself pursuing his studies rather further than he might otherwise have done. Just by chance, or so it might have appeared, he had been simultaneously commissioned to write a feature article for a Washington colour magazine on a number of national societies in the States, and one of the subjects he had chosen to write about was the Federation. What he wanted he had told them when he first wrote approaching them about the article, was a number of interviews with expatriate Scots. These interviews would be illustrated with glossy photographs of such Scottish-American lairds complete with kilts and sheep-dogs, standing in front of their Texas ranches, or New England mansions. More Scottish than the Scots was to be the angle.

So he had approached the Executive of the Federation and had got precisely nowhere. He was surprised at the rejection of his offer to publicise the efforts the Federation said they had been making over the years to help keep Scottish exiles and friends of Scotland in touch with what was going on in the old country. A wall of silence greeted his request for interviews with the leading lights of the Society, so he had to make do with interviewing some of the handful of former office bearers of the Federation. That had started it. Tesco had thought at first that, as with so many voluntary organisations, tribal and personality jealousies had got the upper hand. But such was the unanimity of opinion among these former office bearers about the nature of the new Executive Committee of the Federation, that he soon realised something more fundamental was at fault. So strong was the feeling that the Federation had *gone wrong*, that these ardent Scots who had, in one way or another, been removed from the Federation Executive, were well on the way to setting up a rival body to promote the interests of Scotland in a more traditional way. There was a man called MacPake, the former President of the Federation, there was someone else called Lindsay who was angrily providing the funds. Tesco spent a remarkable number of hours talking to and listening to these men. Then he began to collate his material in a way which, while it did admittedly serve for an article, left him with a vastly greater amount of background on certain aspects of Scottish life in the States and in Scotland than he could possibly use journalistically in the short run.

Now, Tesco was back in Edinburgh, but in a well-established way. An office had been rented at the top of a building just behind Princes Street; he had a young male assistant and a secretary. To those who had known him before it would perhaps be a fraction odd to see that he had set up his own news agency, carefully registered with the Ministry of Trade and Industrial Development. A scrupulous investigator might have wondered at the market for the product of the *Federate Press Agency*, but there was plenty of evidence scattered about the outer office of a glossy gossipy nature, to reassure them about the type of material that the agency itself peddled. That was as it should be. Walt Tesco's young male assistant, a typical all-American boy, went by the name of William T. Sedge. Sedge was his mother's maiden name, the T stood for Torrance, and the boy's father had been killed not very long ago in an odd motor-car accident in Manhattan. The girl secretary was a girl secretary of very minimal accomplishments. She was called Deirdre, and that was as it should be too.

Walt Tesco had been sitting in his back office with William Sedge when the telephone rang. Tesco picked up the receiver; Sedge listened in on the extension earphone.

"It's tonight," said the voice. For Tesco and Sedge there was no need to ask who was calling. "They've got Mockingham already," the voice at the other end of the line went on. "Straight from the hospital. They're earlier than we guessed. They're going out for MacDowall now, so it's too late to get him away. But see what you can do about his daughter, will you?"

Tesco muttered that he'd do what he could, then the voice

broke in again. "I can't ring you again. Special Task Unit told me the police had a tail on me. I lost the man easily for this phone call, but I can't guarantee it every time. I'm going to bury myself for a day or so." There was a click and the phone went dead.

After a moment, Sedge turned to Tesco and burst out: "Well, that's it. We came too late. It's all over and they've won."

"Not at all, not at all," wheezed Walt Tesco enigmatically. "If we can trust that Harvard Business School product, and I believe we can, I think we've just begun."

The previous twenty-four hours brought its own serious disruption into the life of Ealasaid MacDowall. She had been at her new work in the big glass and steel office for the past week, and, by and large, she was enjoying it. Sitting at her rosewood desk in the corner of the big open-plan office, the only changes she had so far introduced were to reposition one or two of the large fleshy indoor plants that stood about the place in order to give herself just a little bit more privacy. It wasn't that she liked the plants, but she did miss the system of everyone with their own office even if it were only a cubicle.

Learning the deceits and jargon of the public relations industry, she was embarked at that moment on her first major exercise, a scenario for selling Bondi tape recorders. She had begun to get into the swing of writing when one of her colleagues, a plump, flashy young man with a penchant for dirty jokes, came across to chat her up. In the process, he made some passing remark about the morning's attempt on the life of the Secretary to the Cabinet. He had just heard the newsflash, he said. Ealasaid didn't register at first, and the young man, unaware of her parentage, went on with his attempted banter with this rather attractive new colleague of his. She cut him short, extracted all he knew with a few terse worried questions, and then reduced him to a blushing embarrassed silence with her explanation. To give him his due, he dismissed from his mind the fact that the pubs had just opened and that he had a drinking engagement with some of his cronies, and offered her a lift to the hospital. By the time they got there, her father had already discharged himself, however, so the plump young man found himself ferrying her on to her father's office to his growing regret, since his sympathy had worn thin in the meantime along with the realisation that he was totally out of her class. Once there, he promptly excused himself and went his way, with a good knight-errant story at least to his credit.

Ealasaid had to wait for a few moments in her father's outer office while he dealt with one of the stream of important well-wishers, but then, unable to restrain herself any more, she burst in to see him. He stood up, and was all smiling and welcoming, though she knew him too well not to realise that there was strain and pain being held back under the surface. In the end she let him convince her that the wound was trifling, that the would-be assassin was almost certainly a crank, and that everything else was going fine. She was consoled at the time, and it was only later that she realised everything couldn't be quite as simple as he had made out.

The rest of the day she spent in routine pursuits, though she didn't return to her office. She met her mother off the plane from Inverness, got her safely ensconced back at the family home, and when she was sure that all was well, left her waiting for her father to return at the end of the day. Then Ealasaid set off to catch a bus back to town. She had a long-standing dinner engagement which, in view of her father's apparent confidence and her mother's fairly relaxed attitude, she felt she could continue to keep without feeling guilty.

The men who came later and took away her mother, found they had misjudged. They put out a big alert after seven forty-five. The instructions were to bring Ealasaid in with her father and mother; there had been very explicit threats about the rewards of failure. The Police Commissioner, a recent disciple of the new cause, whose penchant for law, order and firm government had made him an easy convert, had personally issued the directive.

Ealasaid meanwhile spent a relaxed if tedious evening with her friends in the city outskirts. As they weren't in any way concerned with public life and didn't appear to be aware of the morning's attempt on her father's life, she refrained from imposing her problems on them. By ten-thirty, she excused herself from their suburban gossip and they rang for a taxi to take her back to her flat in the centre.

The taxi dropped her at the end of her street. It was part of a complex one-way system, and had the taxi driven her the whole way round and right to her door, it would have meant quite a lot more on the meter. At the corner where she got out, in the lee of a doorway, stood one of those yellow boxes that newspaper sellers are given by their employers to keep their wares dry and to advertise their paper. A single torn copy of a late evening edition was blowing about on top in the damp evening wind. As she passed, she caught the banner headline *Government Purge*. She stopped, went back and picked up the paper, automatically placing some coins in the box as she did so. She stood there under a streetlight and glanced through the story. It was thin stuff. There were unconfirmed reports of a crisis, of Ministers resigning and officials being dismissed. She saw her father's name mentioned, but not in any definite context. It worried her. She walked on, clutching the newspaper tightly in her hand.

Two policemen were positioned at the door of the block of flats where she lived, talking to the old janitor whose back was towards her. The old man was rather deaf and in the still night air his words carried clearly across the road. After what she had just read, what she now heard made her hesitate for the second time that day, unsure that she could possibly have understood right. The shock of the morning's happenings had made her peculiarly aware of the possibilities of the extraordinary, and the juxtaposition of her own name and the word *arrest*, made her move on an impulse back into the shadow of the houses. She retraced her steps back along the street. Stopping at the corner, she went into a telephone kiosk, and tried to ring her parents. For a full half-minute the ringing tone went unanswered. She was beginning to get worried about waking them so late at night with her absurd doubts and questions, but then there was an unknown male voice on the line confirming that she was on to the right number. She was abruptly asked who was calling. A moment's hesitation, she said nothing and hung up. Cold with fear, for some minutes she stood transfixed in the telephone box, uncertain what to do next. Then nervously she started to look up a number in the directory. It took some time. Eventually she found the number and rang a friend she had on the night editorial staff of the *Scotsman*. When she was put through to him at last, he was obviously taken totally aback. Then he told her. Her father had been arrested. They had just been given a news release, still embargoed, that she was being held for questioning too. What was it all about, he asked? Could she give a personal interview if he sent a journalist? She swore at her former night-editor friend and crashed the receiver down violently. The action jarred her into a more realistic appraisal of her situation.

The sound of a police siren echoed in the night air, and a car's headlights swung round and along the street. A blue light flashed on and off. Instinctively she realised that they might have traced the call to her parents. She wondered if they might indeed be after her, whatever the reason. For a moment rationality argued that she had nothing to fear from the police, even if her father were in some sort of trouble, that she should wait where she was to find out. Then another, stronger instinct made her slip out of the box and into the night. She watched from the shelter of a nearby doorway. The car arrived a moment later; policemen poured from it at once, torches piercing the darkness round the telephone box.

It is remarkable how quickly animal instincts of survival emerge. She was neither sure why they should be looking for her nor why she should be running away. Yet both she and these policemen were acting in this way. And they had told the press that she had been detained.

She moved easily from shadow to shadow, knowing the ground well. Once round a corner and well away from them, she could relax once again. Hesitantly she emerged into the lighted street.

A car pulled into the kerb beside her. A window wound down and someone she couldn't make out hissed "Miss MacDowall?"

She drew back.

"Come on. There's not much time," the voice repeated. "It's you they're after. We're listening in on the police net right now, and they've got the area almost completely cordoned off. Come on. Quickly now. Jump in."

Slowly she moved back towards the car and did what she was told. How had they known her name?

For her father, being arrested was a controlled, undramatic event. He had stayed late at the Office as a result of a message that the Prime Minister wanted to see him at the Residence at eight o'clock. It was rather unthinking of the PM, but MacDowall presumed that the old man, in his growing senility, had already forgotten all about the morning's shooting. Dutiful to the end, and after ringing his wife to tell her he'd be late, MacDowall, now grey with tiredness, waited on as he had been asked. His personal staff had long gone home.

The wave of arrests were perfectly synchronised. It was important to keep publicity down to the minimum possible in the circumstances. Three men came for the Secretary to the Cabinet at seven forty-five precisely. There was no problem. He was alone, restlessly dozing in his chair, and the men were all strangers.

FIFTEEN

IT WAS A perfectly agreeable bedroom and in no way a prison
cell. I had been there since the interview with Carlyle and de
Laski which had ended about mid-day. It was now nearly six
in the evening and quite dark outside. A waiter, complete with
white jacket and black bow tie, had brought me an adequate
meal in my room at lunchtime, and I was promised dinner at
seven. I had a plentiful supply of light reading material in the
room, but had too much to think about for fiction. I had lain
flat on my bed almost without moving since I had finished the
lunch. I had been told not to leave the room without summon-
ing one of the resident guards, and I saw no value in my
indulging in any pointless histrionics.

It had come to me as a cataclysmic shock to discover that
what I had been told was indeed the truth. Only now was I
beginning to force myself to come to terms with it. The day's
developments, from the briefly-held belief that Ingram and
Dobbs had gone mad, through to the realisation that a *coup*
of enormous dimensions had more or less succeeded, was a
stupefying jump, but I had to try to face up to it. With zealous
expertise they had justified to me that what they had said about
the take-over of all the important sectors of the country's
industrial and manufacturing strength was entirely true; in
addition, all major land holdings, property and so on that came
on the market were being bought up by them, perfectly legi-
timately. They were now, by many times, the biggest land-
owners in the country. They were clearly well on the way to
eroding successfully the political fabric of the country and
replacing it, man for man, with their own puppet régime. They
took pains to explain just how far they had gone; how they
were now trying to speed up the process by getting at the
stalwarts, as de Laski had called them, people like myself,

intrinsically powerful yet likely to be difficult to win over, circumvent or corrupt.

They had planned well and it was difficult to see them not succeeding. The simple message to me had been, join us or be removed, one way or another. It was no longer to be by violent means, I was politely told. The attempt to assassinate the Secretary to the Cabinet was, I was assured, arranged and plotted at low level. The Bondi directors had been more than shocked. Violence was out from now on. There was no need. Character assassination was both simpler and cleaner.

For some time I had remained aloof, fascinated yet personally detached from this fantastic exposé, confident of my own moral position and what I must do to expose the scheme if I were permitted to do so. Then they started on me. Calmly and efficiently, they produced documentary evidence of my supposed complicity in the whole operation from the beginning. It came in a neatly-filed dossier of evidence. I was given a copy of my own to take away and study. According to the carefully-arranged papers, I had accepted the offer of aid put to me by Torrance away back at the beginning. If I had genuinely done so it would have made it all the easier for them, since the Bondi Corporation had taken over Torrance's idea almost before he had got round to formulating it himself. Otherwise, de Laski told me, if Torrance had had his way, it might indeed have offered a panacea for the country's ills which would have made their take-over bid all the more difficult. The slant was that in the dossier, a letter apparently signed by Torrance, now of course dead, testified not only that I had accepted, but that, at the same time, I had made it a condition that I be allowed to grease my own palm, filtering off a sizeable sum for my own use. Torrance had bridled at the last bit, and had had to be got rid of. De Laski told me this almost as an aside.

When de Laski had quietly related it all to me, I began to laugh it away, to ridicule it. But then they showed me my private bank statements for the previous year, totally accurate except for large regular monthly payments into my account.

They had laboriously reconstructed my balance with the aid of my bank itself, the manager of which, an old friend of mine, was now also under their tutelage. This little glimpse of unexpected petty corruption shocked me enormously. They had been so painstaking. My personal copies of my bank statements over the same period had been sought out as well, removed from my house, and the new versions substituted. It was all so simple, yet so frighteningly efficient. Everything had been thought of, down to the last detail. Had I not been so numbed by that stage in the revelation, I might well have cracked. They sent me away to think things over.

"You have total freedom of choice, Mr Mockingham," Carlyle had summed up.

"Like Tawney who talked of the freedom a poor man has to dine at the Ritz," I responded with more panache than I felt, or the occasion merited.

"Most agreeable too, Mr Mockingham," was the laconic reply. "The Ritz is pleasant enough."

MacDowall was slouched in a deep armchair and I failed to notice the sling until he stood up to greet me.

"We live in interesting times," he smiled faintly.

"That used to be an ancient Chinese curse," I began. De Laski came in behind me and started talking loudly before I could go any further.

"I'm sorry, gentlemen, that we have had to bring you together in what cannot be entirely relaxed circumstances, but we have, for some peculiar reason of economy, only one television set in this part of the building, and I think that none of us would particularly like to miss the statement. A drink anyone?"

He pressed a bell and a man in a white jacket came in immediately. MacDowall coldly declined the offer, but I had to some degree come to terms with this dream, and I ordered a large whisky and soda.

The intervening hours had passed slowly. Dinner had come

and gone, well served to me in my room. Then, just before nine-thirty, de Laski had come and invited me to watch something on television. It would, he said, be of considerable interest to me in terms of my future. It didn't occur to me to decline. Neither did I attempt to question him on what the programme was about. I could wait.

The set was on with the sound turned down. A cowboy film was in its final throes. The hero, wordless and wounded, was lying in a girl's lap. In the background, some crook was being dragged away by the Sheriff's men. Gradually the scene faded and the titles were superimposed. De Laski went forward and turned up the sound as the programme announcer, whom I knew quite well, came on the screen and announced that the channel, in common with all other radio and television networks at this time, was about to broadcast a special message from the Government. Then, incongruously, they started to play the national anthem.

"Quite a good touch, don't you think?" I heard de Laski whisper in the background. He had addressed his remark to Carlyle who had just reappeared.

The picture faded and came into focus once again, and this time Ian Campbell was on the screen. It was obvious that he was slightly nervous and not over-well prepared. He glanced to one side seeking guidance from some hidden producer as to whether he was yet on the air. Then he turned towards the cameras and began to speak. Haltingly at first, and then more fluently as he began to focus on the teleprompt in front of him. His tie was squint, which added to the nervous uncertainty of his appearance.

"Good evening. I am speaking to you this evening in the aftermath of a great crisis. There have been considerable behind-the-scenes tensions and conflicts that, in a host of evil and unseen ways, were seeking to destroy the whole fabric of our society. Indeed, so organised were these forces, that the whole existence of this country as a state was for some time, in very grave danger." Campbell hesitated for a moment, nervously brushing away a lock of hair from his brow.

"I should also explain at the outset that I am speaking to you as your new Minister of Home Affairs. The Prime Minister, who will be addressing the nation tomorrow, did me the honour of appointing me to this crucial post only this morning, after some very grave facts had been brought to his attention about the holders of some of the highest offices in the State. Full details of these facts are being issued this very evening in the form of a White Paper, which will be available to you free at your local Post Office and at other public offices. I will not, therefore, go into all the sad and disgraceful details here. Suffice it to say that a conspiracy of the very highest order was under way, to subvert the constitution and, it is not too strong to say, to sell this country out to a group of self-seeking, self-motivated men of little or no scruple.

"As a result of information gathered over a number of months by loyal servants of the State, we, the Authorities, have managed to nip this in the bud. This *coup d'état*, and I use the term only with the greatest reluctance since it must sound to you like some melodrama out of the third world, has been thwarted. You will remember that there has been considerable and growing industrial and civil unrest in many parts of the country for a long time now. I am sure I do not have to remind you, for example, of the murder of several members of our security forces, of the blowing up of our transmitters, and of numerous other acts of sabotage and criminal nuisance. I can now reveal that all these incidents were part of a carefully planned and executed plot, which, but for the vigilance of our security forces, would have succeeded.

"You will discover, when you study the White Paper, that many famous names, names synonymous with power in this country, have tragically involved themselves in this gigantic plot. Under the courageous and distinguished leadership of our Prime Minister, these forces of evil have now been uncovered. You will also discover, as you read, that there were other men, less wicked, but weak and misguided; men, I am sad to say,

such as Malcolm Mockingham, the previous holder of the high
and distinguished office which I now hold. He, alas, was one of
these. He is, as you all know, a sick man, and perhaps much of
the root cause of his recent behaviour lies in this physical difficulty. Who are we to judge . . . ?" Campbell paused for a
moment and managed, by so doing, to impart a moment of
partial drama into what he was saying. I took in his words as
if in a dream. For a moment, indeed, I stopped listening. When
I focused again, Campbell had turned to talk about the Secretary to the Cabinet.

". . . all have heard about the dastardly attack on the Secretary to the Cabinet. I can, I think, be sure that I am speaking
for you all when I say how much we deplore such happenings,
and we are, and will continue to make every effort to see that
the culprit is brought to justice. Sir Alexander MacDowall,
I am sorry to tell you, was injured very much more badly than
was at first believed, but there is still hope, and while there is
hope . . ." I glanced across at the subject of this sick parody.
MacDowall was sitting slouched in his chair, eyes almost
closed, unmoving. I knew and appreciated that here was someone far from sick, someone very much alert. He had too great
a reputation, he was too well known and trusted to be branded
either as one of the evil men behind the affair, or one of those
too weak or self-seeking to avoid disaster, like me. I sat up
sharply at the thought, anger welling inside me with such force
as I had never known before. I pushed down with my hands
on the arms of the wheelchair, and, for a moment, I realised,
that I could have stood up unaided. I knew it for a fact, though
I didn't straighten myself the whole way. Then I fell back
into the seat again with the knowledge that I really had im-
proved my condition. In its strange way, this shock made my
mind all the more alert to the danger that I now was in. I
glanced down at my hands; the knuckles were white as they
still gripped round the arms. It took some moments and considerable cramp pains before I could relax my hands.

This very personal event, if I thought about it, seemed to

have lasted for several minutes. But when I came to, I realised that only a few seconds had passed and that, almost certainly, no one had noticed. They were all intent on listening to Ian Campbell, former Governor of the Reserve Bank, now Minister of Home Affairs.

"We have therefore felt it necessary, and with great reluctance, to introduce internment and martial law. The police will have the power to act in a wider and regrettably more all-embracing way than has been the rule heretofore. I have instructed that they be issued with arms; they have orders to shoot on sight if their lawful commands are not obeyed or if they otherwise need so to act in the execution of their duty. Again, full details of these new regulations are contained in the Government's White Paper which is published this evening.

"I can assure you that at the very first moment it becomes possible, we will remove all these new and unfortunate regulations from the statute book. This is a free and democratic country. We must try to safeguard this inheritance. Good night and God bless you all."

The picture faded and we were left looking at a blank, flickering screen. I think even Carlyle and de Laski were rather overawed by the broadcast, though they must certainly have had a large hand in its drafting. Then the announcer was on the screen again, introducing, so he said, a full and special programme of news on the day's dramatic events. There followed a television report of the events leading up to the crisis. It had obviously been specially prepared well in advance. Film of the Clydebank riots followed with flashbacks to the blowing up of the radio transmitter. There was a reconstruction of the attempted assassination of MacDowall, backed up by today's film of arrests of certain top political suspects, of myself leaving hospital this morning, *under the armed guard*, according to the report, of Dobbs and Ingram. Surely this sort of stuff wouldn't fool anyone who knew me? But it was so well and convincingly done. Expert film editors had been employed and it was, in presentation, a most competently-made propaganda film. Again my hands were straining at the arms of my wheelchair.

The final film shots were of the formation of the new Government by the Prime Minister. There were several scenes of him, carefully chosen to indicate his serious concern and to avoid those glimpses which might give away his vacant senility to the credulous public. All the while, the commentator was pouring out insidious stuff about how deep the rot had gone, how the Prime Minister had been forced to appoint to high office people like Ian Campbell who, though not elected MPs, had in their previous service to the State, demonstrated their abiding loyalty. Campbell, it was announced, would be adopted for a seat as soon as one came vacant, and the wait would not be all that long, since a further Government decree precluded interned individuals from continuing to remain members of the National Assembly.

On and on it went, myth after fiction, until even I did not know what or what not to believe. There were parts of the programme that were totally genuine, sections on the economic state of the country, for example, which had been inserted to give those who might harbour suspicions, certain undeniable facts on which to cut their doubts short. If you're going to lie, lie big.

Then Carlyle was talking, standing up, turning the television sound down once again. He said he imagined we had all had enough. The lights in the room were turned up. I blinked and moved my head to look at MacDowall. He looked as if he hadn't moved; motionless, eyes like slits behind his half-moon spectacles. Yet again I was aware of a much more alert brain than mine working overtime underneath; I reckoned that Carlyle and his colleagues appreciated this only too well.

"We have unfortunately to keep you under close confinement, Sir Alexander," said Carlyle, as if reading my thoughts. "You will appreciate how inevitable that is." He smiled benignly. MacDowall didn't react.

Turning to me, Carlyle added: "You, Mr Mockingham, are

your own best captive." He looked pointedly down at my legs. "By the way, you'll now appreciate why we were reluctant to accept Torrance's estimate of Ian Campbell's likely role in affairs." I felt again that blind surge of anger at the unpleasantness of the man. But this time, I knew that I had managed to control it, that almost nothing of what I was feeling showed. I was learning both from the Secretary to the Cabinet and from my own mental and physical pain that nothing was to be gained by displaying my emotions.

"One other point I should add. You, Mr Mockingham, have just one close relative, your wife. I understand that she is now pursuing her wayward way down in London. I don't upset you by talking in this way? No, I thought not. There is little trouble to be expected in that direction. I believe you haven't heard from her for some considerable time." Carlyle paused briefly, rang for the waiter and ordered another drink. This time I refused. He was right. Mention of my wife affected me not at all.

"But for you, Sir Alexander, I'm afraid things are rather different." Carlyle spoke slowly and deliberately. MacDowall gave the first signs of movement he had shown since the television programme had begun. Shifting slightly in his chair, he opened his eyes a fraction, adjusted his rimless glasses on the centre of his long nose and stared intensely over them at Carlyle. Even in these one-sided circumstances, the look was a powerful one, one that had been known to scare lesser men rigid. Carlyle hesitated for a moment and then turned away to continue with what he was saying.

"You are a closely-knit family, and that spells danger. You will understand, therefore, our reasons for putting your wife and daughter under, shall we call it, *protective custody* pending your, er, good behaviour."

Despite his arm in its sling, MacDowall uncoiled himself from his seat with lightning rapidity and advanced on Carlyle, eyes burning. Immediately the waiter and another white-capped American guard appeared, both armed, and MacDowall was roughly pushed back and away out of Carlyle's range. It was a tense situation, all the more so because no words were spoken. Then it was all over, and MacDowall resumed his seat. But his eyes were wider open now and he was watching Carlyle like a hawk.

"To continue, Sir Alexander, if I may . . ." Carlyle tried to appear sarcastic, but he had been rattled by the sudden threat of violence, and it didn't quite come off. "Your wife and daughter are well and comfortably housed in another building in this complex. I'm afraid that until things have settled down a bit we can't let you get together. But I hope that in a few days . . ."

"If the slightest thing happens to them . . ." MacDowall, despite himself, let out a hissed, unfinished remark. It would have been all too effective in normal circumstances, but these were far from normal.

"I can assure you that that depends entirely on you. They are, if you like, hostages to your good behaviour." Carlyle smiled unctuously, bowed slightly to MacDowall and then said: "Now I'm afraid I can't leave you two together for the moment. This thing is in its very earliest of stages, as you will appreciate, and we can't have the opposition, even if they are, shall we call it, castrated, getting together to conspire against us in the very moment of our triumph."

No one spoke, and once again, for a brief moment, Carlyle looked nonplussed. Perhaps he expected some congratulations from us in this moment of his triumph as he called it, since it was all too obviously an overwhelmingly important occasion for him. Then he looked round at de Laski, regained his self-composure, smiled and, in a brisk voice, said: "To your rooms, Gentlemen. *To your rooms.*"

SIXTEEN

"ALL RIGHT, YOU can go, Mr Mockingham."

"I beg your pardon?" It was seven in the morning and I was hardly awake.

"You can leave; go home. You're free. There'll be a car to pick you up in one hour. Please be ready."

De Laski turned and left the room, and I sat up in bed. What was going on? I had been a virtual prisoner for nearly three days, three days of enforced idleness, speaking to no one, seeing no one except for the man who brought my food and helped me when I wanted to wash and so on. Since that evening round the television set listening to my successor's broadcast, I hadn't set eyes on de Laski or Carlyle, let alone MacDowall. It had left me all the time I wanted to think about what it all meant. Such contemplation hadn't got me very far. Now I was being told I could leave, go away. Go away where? Unless it was all some sort of ridiculous joke, I was not going back to my previous life.

The man who waited on me came in with a breakfast tray, and announced that he had been told to help me pack my things. That was a minimal task. My lack of everything except what I had had with me in hospital had been one of the more irritating factors in my captivity. I questioned the man, but he would say or knew nothing. I dressed myself and the hour passed. De Laski reappeared.

"Where am I going?" I asked lamely.

"Your personal possessions have been moved from your former official residence and are now at your own house in your former constituency." He gave exceptional stress to the use of the word former. We had kept our old house, my wife and I, sometimes going back to it for a quiet week-end in election times, and on holiday. But in recent months and with

nothing of a home life left to me, it had remained empty apart
from a woman from the village who came to air it occasionally.

"Your housekeeper, Mrs Ingram, has moved in. We've
arranged everything. Her husband, as you'll be aware, is in
our employ, and he'll be living there as well. Ingram, assisted
by some of our security men, will see that you conform. You
are to have no visitors, at least until things settle down a bit."

"House arrest?" My mouth felt dry. I could have done without the Ingrams.

"Sort of. In your physical condition, despite your . . . er
. . . downfall, the public probably wouldn't take kindly to you
being kept in close confinement."

"You're surely not worried about the public—you don't take
account of democracy still, do you?"

"Quite right," said de Laski briefly. "There's no room for
democracy in big business; that's all this is, you see. But we still
have to keep the shareholders happy, so to speak, and there's
a lot of sympathy about for you, despite our efforts. As I said,
your accident . . ."

"You needn't go on. You've made yourself abundantly
clear." I turned my head away, to hide my anger more than
anything else.

"Very well. Goodbye, Mr Mockingham. We may meet again
sometime. It may be useful for us to resuscitate your image at
some future date. We may be able to find a job for you. Oh,
by the way, you'll have some money paid you regularly. Again,
the public . . ." He paused, and smiled unpleasantly. "*Care and
maintenance basis* we call it in the Bondi Corporation."

It was one of the cheaper Fords, and I had difficulty getting
into the back. Ingram appeared and helped me. I couldn't
bring myself to look at him, but I sensed his unease. There
was another man, one of the security people—young, clean cut,
eyes too closely set for much intelligence, a former New York
cop at a guess.

Ingram drove; my guard sat in the front passenger seat.

It was good to have some fresh air, though it was bitterly cold, with something in the wind that was neither thick mist nor yet fine rain. It's frequently there at that time of year. The drive took only three-quarters of an hour, and I feasted my eyes on the countryside as I passed, searching desperately for something that just wasn't evident. That was the odd thing. In the few villages we passed through, there was absolutely no sign of change whatsoever.

It was, without doubt, the longest three months of my life. They didn't tell me in advance that I wouldn't be allowed newspapers, television or radio. There were to be no visitors, and though I have always been a self-contained man, I was to miss desperately having anyone intelligent to talk to. I did have my books, and I had started jotting down a few personal reminiscences as well; it was hardly a diary, since I felt I was a little young to be starting seriously on the memoirs game. I also spent a lot of time working on a study I had always promised myself to undertake when I had the time. This was on the theories of one of the early Scottish economists, John Law, who was responsible, among other things, for founding the Bank of France. He wasn't very successful in following his schemes through, and I felt some sympathy with him. I didn't get much further than making copious notes on index cards, but it kept my mind occupied.

A partial exception to my solitude was that the local minister, a clergyman of the Church of Scotland, an elderly, gangling, half-wit of a man, was, unfortunately, allowed to visit me as part of his pastoral duties. I could have done without. Even if he had possessed the intellect, the surroundings in which his calls took place, with one of my guards sitting on a stiff-backed chair at the door of my study, were more akin to those of prison visiting. The clergyman, in every way convinced of my guilt, and obviously treating his calls precisely as if they were on a prisoner, took it upon himself to try to persuade me to atone; he had the infuriating habit of leaving me with choice phrases about repenting while there was still time. I began to wonder whether his visits were allowed by my captors as some peculiar mental torture.

But there was one joy which, during these months, I believed I managed to keep a secret. Slowly and painfully, both feeling and strength returned in some measure to my legs. I exercised them constantly, morning and night. I remember the excitement when I managed, one evening in my bedroom, to stand almost upright, holding on to the end of my bed like grim death. The process was normally uncomfortable rather than painful, but one morning, after some two months of house arrest, I woke in considerable agony. With some special pleading, my guards, after checking with higher authority, ungraciously arranged for my specialist, Professor Taller, to come over from the hospital to examine me.

Taller was a blunt, red-haired Glaswegian, the son of a Clydeside shipyard welder, who had, in the best tradition, struggled his way through University the hard way. He was a man with few obvious social graces and no bedside manner apparent to the untrained eye, but I had always got on well with him, and we had developed a fairly bluff, good-humoured relationship since the attack had first brought me in as his patient.

That day he had been allowed to come on the strict understanding that he was to restrict himself to clinical questions. But as he was an uncomplex man with a temper and style of his own, surely aware that all could not be as simple as it seemed, these restrictions galled him. I could see as soon as he came in the door that he disliked the whole situation, and I sensed his professional proprieties were severely offended. From the beginning the American security guard was there. When Taller wanted to begin to examine me, he curtly asked the man to leave. The request was met with a blunt refusal. Taller rose on his mettle. He was heavily built, he swore and threatened to throw the guard out. The man withdrew rapidly to seek instructions. The minutes were precious.

"Thank Christ for that," said Taller in a low-toned growl. "He was getting on my bloody wick. Now then, let me see. I think you'll be standing on your own feet by now, and walking fairly soon. Is that not so?" The way he said it, it was more a statement than a question.

I hesitated, then said: "I'd like to think so."

"Well, I'm sixty per cent sure. The operation certainly wasn't a total failure. But you won't want them all to know, I'm thinking." He sounded pleased.

I nodded slowly.

"I never believed the half of what they said about you. I still don't." Taller was keeping his voice well down. "You needn't worry. I'll not be telling anyone about the legs. You may need them sooner than you think. I was asked to tell you if I saw you alone that there are . . ."

At that moment the door burst open and in came the guard with one of the senior American security officers. There was a nasty scene, but eventually Professor Taller had no alternative but to finish his examination of me in angry silence. At the end he was ushered out, leaving me with part of a sentence to brood over.

There was little else in these weeks to relieve the monotony. I rose early each day out of a fear of going physically or mentally stale. I was well enough looked after by Ingram and his silent wife, the money arrived regularly to pay the house-keeping, and in outward ways there was every sign of total normality. Mrs Ingram's cooking was, if anything, even more atrocious than I remembered it, but that failed to disturb me any more. On days when it was especially bad, I simply drank more than the fair quantity I consumed on normal days. The drinking hardly mattered when there was no work to interrupt my hangovers the following morning. I had a good wine cellar and several crates of whisky which came back to me from the Edinburgh house; besides it killed time as well as the pain in my legs. One thing I think I learned during these months was to control my temper once again, something that had got so much out of hand since my incapacity. There was little to be angry about. I neither complained nor attempted to speak to either of the Ingrams nor to the other mainly American guards who appeared on duty, nor did any of them attempt or offer to speak to me. Ingram's guilty looks gradually wore off, giving way to a general all-pervading sullenness.

Apart from the brief unsatisfactory visit of Professor Taller and the embarrassing calls by the dreadful Church of Scotland clergyman, there were only one or two incidents that I remember being of any significance during my house arrest. It is difficult to imagine the experience, since a prisoner in normal circumstances is usually allowed newspapers and radio, but I had absolutely no idea whatsoever of what was going on in the outside world. I was existing in a total news vacuum.

One evening, however, having spent a fairly industrious day going through the material I had had available in my library about the eventual downfall of John Law, I decided to go through to the kitchen, which was on a level with my ground-floor study, to get Mrs Ingram to make me some coffee. The kitchen was empty, but on the table was a parcel of groceries, with, wrapped round some of the vegetables, part of a copy of the previous day's *Scotsman*. I reached over and pulled it clear, crumpled it into a ball, and stuffed it down beside the cushion of my wheelchair just as Mrs Ingram returned. She didn't seem to notice my childish embarrassment as I over-hastily asked for the coffee. I then went back in high excitement to my room and spent the next hour avidly reading every smallest item in the three or four dirty and crumpled pages I had managed to grab. Yet it was interesting how much of a picture I was able to build up, even from the one day's selective news. The front page was missing, but I had the leader and correspondence columns and it is remarkable what these reveal about the things that are really attracting the attention of the public.

The main editorial was on the subject of unemployment. It read oddly. The flat, uncritical commentary on what the Government were doing to better matters, reminded me of some public relations press hand-out. There was nothing there. The second leader, unbelievable as it seemed, was a justification of a moratorium on the activities of all political parties. Had this really been implemented? And if so, did it only deserve a second leader? But perhaps it was old news by now. The public would be bored by repetition. The third leader was about the first cuckoo, so some things hadn't changed.

The letters, the few articles and the news items of significance allowed me to build up what turned out to be a fairly accurate picture of what had been going on. It was like doing a cross-word puzzle.

The picture that emerged was, quite simply, that of a police state. There had been a *coup d'état*, followed by a purge of those who had been in the previous administration, those who were not prepared to perjure themselves. It was in the best tradition of *coups*, the only differences being that it hadn't happened in Africa or South America, but here, and that the motivation wasn't ideological nor even, strictly speaking, political. Neither Communism nor Fascism nor anything in the political spectrum in between, but big business, the Bondi Corporation.

The mechanisms of the *coup* had been fairly bloodless, though there were a few dead policemen and other violences on the way. Instead of a take-over by force, the tactics of *the enemy within* had been adopted. Men had been bought, bribed, black-mailed or, like me, discredited and then discarded.

The very fact that the *coup* was not political but commercial meant that the difficulties had not been experienced during the process of obtaining control from the relatively few that pos-sessed it, but in selling the change in political terms to the public at large. The silent majority had to be brought, through careful propaganda, to accept that there had been a change of power without resort to the ballot-box or elections. What had, at all costs, to be hidden from them was that the country had been the subject of a gigantic take-over bid. That would be too much, if they ever came to realise it.

My reading of these few sheets of crumpled newspaper appeared to indicate that the leaders such as de Laski and Carlyle had rather underestimated this aspect. It was outside their normal experience of take-over bids. Things must have got somewhat out of hand, and this had led to the belated appearance of the more normal symbols of a *coup*, such as the denial, justified on security grounds, of any political activities outside the Government machine. The moratorium on political activity I had read about in the *Scotsman* leader, seemed to extend, though here I was reading between the lines, to the effective stifling of activity in the National Assembly as well. I was to discover later that I had guessed correctly, and that the National Assembly, again on security grounds, had been ordered into indefinite recess.

To judge from the *Scotsman*'s business and Stock Exchange reports, the commercial life of the country was going on much as before, though there seemed to have been certain tax changes relating to company practice, which, I was to discover, were introduced at the considerable expense of those firms and industries that were not yet part of the Bondi Corporation complex.

There were large gaps in the picture I was able to build up from these few inches of newsprint. The police had obviously been won over, or at least their leadership had. But what of the other services of the State, the small but well-equipped army, the intelligence services, the Special Task Unit, the Civil Service itself? Was everything working so smoothly? Just because the leaders had changed, was the infrastructure carrying on obediently as if nothing had happened? I was left to guess. The small print, the reports of stoppages and lock-outs, suggested considerable industrial unrest, but that was no new thing. It really would have been surprising if such things had disappeared overnight. Then, and most importantly, how was it all being presented and accepted internationally? Because the news and information media were totally State-controlled, was the truth getting outside any more than it was getting through to the public at home?

When I felt I had extracted as much from the newspaper as I could in the circumstances, I folded the sheets carefully and hid them in the pages of a book. And then, I remember, I put aside the ice-cold coffee that had stood forgotten on my desk, and poured myself four fingers of Scotch.

It was later that same evening. I was finishing my exercises and preparing for bed when I heard the noise at my bedroom window. I had lived all these weeks at ground level and at first I dismissed the sound, thinking it was a mouse or one of the guards doing his tedious night rounds. But then again there was a regular tapping and I decided to investigate. Laboriously I moved myself from the floor where I had been exercising, back into my wheelchair. I moved more slowly than I needed, so that if, by any chance, a guard was watching me through the curtains, he would not see me more active and fit than I wanted them to believe I was.

I wheeled myself cautiously over to the window. There was a pause in the tapping. I waited. It came again, and I eased the curtains apart. It wasn't particularly bright in my room, and at first I could not see anything against the darkness of the night. Then gradually I made out the silhouette of a man's hand, peculiarly white in the half-light; it appeared at the window sill in a gesture beckoning me to open up. I froze for what seemed an age, not knowing what to expect. Then my wheelchair must have slipped a little, for I was still gripping the curtains, and the movement caused them to open wider than I had intended. For an instant, a beam of light lit up the man's face. It was a young face, a bad complexion framed in long streaky hair. He looked startled and then, almost at once, there was the sound of a shot. I have this vivid, lasting impression, still with me when I shut my eyes and remember, of his mouth opening in a surprised rather than agonised soundless cry of death, and then of the blotchy face, the heavy head of hair, slowly disappearing, sinking from view below the level of the window-sill. I looked out, and could see nothing. A

guard came in to the room behind me and ordered me away
from the window. I did as I was told, undressed and went to
bed. But sleep didn't come easily that night. I heard the confused shouting outside, the sound of a car being driven up and
the American Guard Commander's voice, authoritative, telling
unseen men to be careful and not to get blood over everything.

In the morning, the gravel outside my window had been
freshly raked.

Again a long time passed and there was nothing. I worked
on John Law. But I ran out of enthusiasm, then out of material,
and they said they couldn't arrange to get the references I needed
from the National Library. I was told it might be different later.
So I started reading fiction. I read a great deal. I never heard
anything about the man who had been shot, and in my limbo
I didn't want to know. Workmen came one day and put strands
of barbed wire along the top of the high wall that surrounded
the garden. A caravan arrived to house the guards in more
comfort at a vantage point beside the front drive. They also
fitted up some floodlights, but never got round to getting them
to work.

I had been indulging in a bout of Scott's novels and had
just finished *Ivanhoe*. It wasn't deep literature, but that too
suited my mood, and the thing that kept me going was that
my legs were coming into their own again. At times it was hell.
The pain was intense. I resorted to a mixture of recourse to the
bottle and to overdosing myself with some pills Professor
Taller had left behind. He said he would come to give me
another check-up, but he never materialised. Only later I discovered that he too was a prisoner; but he was less fortunate
in Peterhead Jail.

I exhausted myself with discreet exercising. One evening in
particular I reached a peak of triumph, standing for a moment,
unaided. Then I forced a movement of my legs which, to me,
was as good as a guardsman's step. It drained me of energy
and filled me with elation. I did something I had done too often

of late. I poured myself whiskies in quick and joyful celebration. I finished a whole bottle of my rapidly diminishing stock. Coupled with the pills it had a devastating effect, for later that night, I nearly went back to stage one. In the height of my spirited, solitary celebrations, I tried the walking feat once again and ended by crashing drunkenly on the floor. As I fell, I remember that the metal brake handle of my wheelchair caught my trousers and tore them, ripping a superficial gash in my leg. There was a lot of blood.

The crash brought in Ingram and his wife. They were greeted by my being violently sick on the floor and it took some time before they had cleared up and got me to bed. I felt remote and must have produced a lot of drugged or drunken chatter. They started talking to each other openly, sure in the knowledge that I wouldn't understand or remember what they were saying. But as they left and shut the door, and just before I passed into an alcoholic oblivion, I clearly heard Mrs Ingram say fiercely:

"It would have to happen like this tonight of all nights."

Perhaps one in the morning: the Ingrams were back and had me half-dressed before I was even vaguely awake. I felt dreadful; the hour or so's sleep had removed the superficial effect of the pills, but the bottle of whisky had left me with the beginnings of a drastic hangover. As I came to, I experienced a strong feeling of nausea. Then I put it into practice. Mrs Ingram responded with remarkable calm and with a cupful of what might have been Bovril out of a thermos flask. My leg ached where I had fallen. What the hell did they think they were doing? I started to roar out complaints, but was immediately stilled by a fierce imprecation from Ingram.

"Get a bloody grip. Keep quiet. Don't you bloody understand, you drunken . . . *Christ!* Why does he have to do it tonight?" It was odd how white and strained he looked. Almost as if he were afraid. The woman was much more composed.

Another man had appeared out of nowhere. I didn't recognise him at first, then gradually, the dreadful old clergyman from the local church came into focus. I started to say something rude, to swear at him, but a further bout of sickness overwhelmed me. By the time I had recovered, the mood had passed, and I was dressed. The clergyman had taken off his heavy black overcoat and wide-brimmed clerical hat. Were they going to put the hat on me? I hadn't worn one for years.

"Are we going out?" I burped intelligently. Being sick had helped a little.

"Give him more of that broth," Ingram growled at his wife. "We have to get him sober enough to keep quiet." A further cup of hot Bovril was forced at me. I tried to refuse, but they insisted. It burnt my mouth, and that helped as well.

"What the hell are you on about?" I shouted.

"Quiet." Ingram's voice was hoarse. The clergyman frowned slightly.

"Don't you . . . ?"

"Shall we gag him?" Ingram asked. "We could hide it with a scarf."

"Why not try to explain," the clergyman said quietly. "Wouldn't it be worth trying? That was the plan after all."

Ingram began talking to me in low, urgent tones. I couldn't grasp what he was on about. My head was throbbing.

Then I focused. They were taking me away. I was to escape. It had been planned for weeks. The shooting outside my window those weeks ago had been an amateur first attempt. That had been before Ingram and his wife had been enlisted, before the old buffoon of a clergyman had been brought in to help. It came out then and later. Neither of the Ingrams had been happy about their role as jailers. Apart from anything else they hated living in the country and despite their problems in the past, they had felt grossly disloyal to me. It was nice to hear, though I neither believed it nor gave it much weight at first. Later I knew differently. Ingram had been down to the village. The Church of Scotland clergyman, knowing precisely what was wanted, had got into conversation. There hadn't exactly been a meeting of minds, since Ingram was neither religiously inclined nor the bravest of individuals, but employing the old method of involving him little by little, he had been persuaded to make a virtue out of necessity. But he wasn't a brave man. The clergyman, on the other hand, was. He had long been one of the loyalist members of the General Assembly of the Church, and despite, or perhaps because of, his age and appearance, had been brought in to help me escape. No one could possibly suspect an elderly churchman of being in any way involved.

All that detail came afterwards. There was no time for further explanations now, nor was my mind up to it. The fact that I had become such a vegetable over the past months made me incurious and unquestioning over where I was going and why—indeed if their story was genuine at all. The method of my departure became the all-important, all-painful essential. They were going to carry me out, but upright, as if I were walking, as if I were the clergyman. That I was walking would be the best disguise of all. The guards knew I was confined to a wheelchair. That was why, apart from the Ingrams, there was only one man on at the house and one at the gate. I had an inbuilt prison, so they were there more as a matter of form, and to keep outsiders away.

They had gone to considerable lengths to devise the escape. There was a sort of yoke and harness. I was to suspend myself between the Ingrams, my legs hanging uselessly below in simulation of walking. Mrs Ingram was a fairly big woman but I felt she wouldn't be able to carry me for long.

They put on the clerical hat and the coat. Then they propped me back on my bed, and the clergyman sat down in my wheelchair. I stared at them stupidly as the Ingrams started tying him into the chair. Then they gagged him. He was an old man. He would be able to tell the guards later that he hadn't had the strength to resist. The Ingrams came back to me with the harness. They said they had been practising. It would be quite easy. They put the metal yoke across their shoulders and came

each side of my bed. Fighting back a new bout of nausea I
linked my arms through the harness. They lifted me. My feet
dragged across the floor. In the darkness it would look like
three people walking in line abreast.

We struggled sideways through the door into the hall,
leaving the old man in my chair. The hat fell off and rolled on
to the carpet. They left it where it lay. There wasn't time.
Outside it was pitch-dark; the full moon was obscured by the
clouds and there was a slight drizzle. Out of the door and
across the drive towards a parked car. My feet trailed limply,
rattling across the gravel. I felt a gripping pain in my legs
which for a moment or two offset the hangover.

A torch shone faintly from the caravan by the drive and the
guard on duty shouted something, Ingram shouted out that he
was driving the clergyman home. It was as simple as that. Or
nearly. Getting into the car was a problem, but we approached
it from the side facing away from the guard, and having assured
himself that nothing was amiss, he lost interest and returned to
the warmth of the caravan. There were one or two hectic
minutes of struggle in the darkness, and then we were all in
and away. The car with Ingram at the wheel pulled down the
drive and hooted at the gate. The guard came out and opened
up. He hardly gave us a glance. I left house arrest after nearly
three months.

SEVENTEEN

ONE OF THE greatest pleasures was the return of newspapers into my life. The other was having people to talk to again. There was a lot to catch up with.

In other ways Ravenscliff was much less comfortable, since the administrative machinery of running the place was rudimentary. I had been well looked after during my house arrest, and here orders were to keep indoors and strictly out of sight. Ravenscliff was a large Georgian house, a pleasant grey stone building, some seven miles south of the Border. Up a long secluded drive in the hills, it stood well hidden among thick plantations of Forestry Commission trees.

Ingram and his wife deposited me, sick and exhausted, at something like five in the morning, before themselves driving further south. Fortunately Independence hadn't led to immigration controls at the border, and only the Customs were involved at the checkpoint at Carter Bar, so there was no difficulty getting into England. A young man I had never seen before met me, and he and Ingram carried me to a room and left me on a bed. Exhausted with drink and the drive, I lapsed into eight or nine hours' deep sleep.

I woke feeling surprisingly fit and excessively curious. The memories and happenings of the previous night came back slowly. I remembered particularly the old clergyman being tied and gagged helplessly in my wheelchair. Flat on my back in the comfort of my bed I surveyed my room. It was bare except for a table on which stood a suitcase containing some of my belongings. The Ingrams must have brought it; something else I had no recollection of. I sat up in bed. The night's journey had done some good and the expected continuation of the hangover didn't materialise. I swung the bedclothes back and dangled my legs over the side of the bed. Most important of all—was this my imagination? I lowered myself gently on to my feet, keeping my balance with both hands on the bed until I was sure that my legs would support my weight. Slowly I moved one leg and then the other. So it was still true. I hadn't imagined it, nor hurt myself too badly when I had fallen.

I started to laugh with joy, and was still giggling to myself when Ealasaid MacDowall came into the room. She was carrying a breakfast tray. She saw me standing unaided and smiled, as if it were the most natural thing in the world.

Later she explained. We were sitting together in what had been the Ravenscliff library. Its fitted oak shelves were still there but empty, except for a few bound and battered volumes of *Punch* and the *Illustrated London News*. It now served as an operations centre. Only a few old tables and chairs, linoleum on the floor, but a modern television set stood in the corner beside a powerful looking short-wave radio transmitter. The abandoned, dust-laden feeling of the room had been cheered up by a fresh bunch of newly-cut flowers on the mantelpiece. The spacious, uncurtained windows looked out on equally spacious, totally unkempt grounds. But it was better than nothing, and they were hardly in a position to complain about having the free use of Ravenscliff by courtesy of Lindsay, the Alabama laird, who owned it. He had never been there and had volunteered its use for the cause.

Ealasaid started to bring me up to date. I tried hard to concentrate, but it would take time, and we both realised it. She poured me cup after cup of black coffee and that helped. After about half an hour, a man came in and joined us. A most unlikely man, Walt Tesco.

It took minutes before I recognised him. He was the journalist, the man who had broken the news of Torrance's death at the New York cocktail party. I remembered giving him the brush-off when he had suggested that it hadn't been an accident. I started to explain.

"Don't give it a thought," Tesco said, beaming charitably from behind thick-lensed spectacles. "It was a bit abrupt of me I must admit. But I've always had a rather suspicious turn of mind. It's essential in gutter journalism. You see", he went on contentedly, "I have no inflated ideas about my profession."

"Walt has been great," Ealasaid interrupted. "He got me out in the nick of time. They tried to buy me. I actually started working for them you know, then they decided to pull me in in any case, because of my father. Walt's now running this end of a sort of Scarlet Pimpernel operation. He fixed up your escape, and even went out and got you your new wheelchair."

"I'm most . . ." I began, but Tesco cut me short.

"I'm only the catalyst," he said a fraction glibly, as if he had just discovered the word. "I'm doing a job, and I get paid for it. A mercenary, but I hope in the best sense of the term. And, well, I suppose I'm not totally uncommitted now either."

He explained that he had been enlisted back in New York by a group of American-Caledonian Loyalists. MacPake and Lindsay were the leading lights. With their financial backing, he had set up and worked from an office in Edinburgh for a few weeks, but he wasn't a professional spy and the Bondi authorities had got too close on one or two occasions. It had been enough time to organise only a rudimentary network, and, much discouraged, he had been on the point of leaving for England when they had had a breakthrough. Tesco had been given, as assistant, William Torrance's son and it had been through him that the information started flooding in.

"We're still getting it. A flood of stuff; all the Cabinet papers, economic and political forecasts, everything of any importance," Tesco said proudly.

"But how did Torrance's son get in on this?" I asked. I remembered his father talking about him during our flight together to New York.

"Martin got in touch with him, and that's the channel still. Torrance Junior acts as courier through to us," Ealasaid broke in.

"Who's Martin?"

"Martin Guthrie."

"*Guthrie.* But how does he . . . ?" I was astounded at the news.

"He's simply carrying on as he did before. He's now Campbell's Private Secretary."

"Incredible . . ."

". . . but true. Though it's extremely dangerous. He'd have had it if they found out."

"And Guthrie is your only source of information?"

"Well no. There's also the Special Task Unit," said Tesco.

"How the hell do you know about them? Their very existence was meant to be known only to a very few and . . ." I began. "I suppose that hardly matters now."

"But it does," Tesco continued, as if he had been involved for years. "You remember that they were a very small unit— only about thirty men in all. They were answerable only to you, to the Secretary to the Cabinet and to the PM. But the PM is just an old fool and had obviously forgotten all about them. So the simple fact is that the Bondi machine slipped up in its take-over bid: it just didn't know they existed."

"The Special Task Unit has been floating about since the *coup* with no status?" I asked.

"They did for a bit. But the Head of the Unit wasn't at a loss for long. He got through to Ealasaid's father, who has been held all the time at Bondi Headquarters, the house where you were first taken. It was a relatively easy job getting access; they're professionals after all. Sir Alexander gave them the gist of what had happened and ordered them to seek out and give support to any movement which might be being set up outside the country with the aim of toppling the Bondi régime. We fell heir to a very experienced mini-intelligence service."

"And now?"

"Now we've got a big, and I hope synchronised, release operation under way. I've just heard that Sir Alexander is out. He's due to arrive here any moment. There are about a dozen others so far; mainly your former colleagues," Tesco explained.

"We're on our way," Ealasaid said excitedly. "It's almost more stimulating than the independence campaign itself. The opposition, the Federalists, weren't malign. This time, there really are some evil specimens about. The Quislings are the worst. In some ways the American big businessmen aren't so bad. They're just doing what they've always done: common commercial practice."

"What are the plans? What are you going to do?"

Tesco was sitting quietly whittling at a pencil. "Until yesterday," he said, "it was all under wraps. Campbell, Carlyle, de Laski and the rest of them had no more than a glimpse of what we'd been doing, what had been going on. You see, while, as you know, they had remarkable success in taking over the top echelons of your Government, the Army and Police, they haven't ever entirely succeeded in winning over the Civil Service, the intelligence and security services. That's quite apart from the Special Task Unit. Loyalty is a strange thing. So are the gaps in Bondi efficiency. When there's a change in a normally-elected democratic government, civil servants change with the facility of a Vicar of Bray. You get the same grey men nationalising and denationalising, selling arms to Fascist régimes and then, equally conscientiously, organising sanctions against the self-same Governments. But this time it's different. Perhaps we'll be less likely to shrug our shoulders when we read of *coups d'état* in African and Asian countries in future."

"And now?" I asked.

"Over the last twenty-four hours, as I said, some twelve former top people have been sprung," Tesco went on. "That's certainly enough to make Campbell and the others sweat. We now go into stage two, the come-back. But we've got to act fast."

"Where do I come in?"

"You've fully recovered? I hear you were hardly yourself last night. The Ingrams were quite upset, and you nearly spoiled things," Tesco said. I made a face, and Ealasaid smiled. "The idea was that you'd be in charge."

"In charge?"

"Good, we knew you'd agree." Ealasaid broke in sweetly.

"If you'd like to sit at this desk and read yourself back into business, you'll be in a better position to take the chair at this afternoon's meeting." Tesco turned brisk.

"What meeting?" I was bewildered. A phone rang and Tesco paused to answer it.

"Call it the Cabinet in Exile if you like," Ealasaid explained, standing up.

"You must excuse us." Tesco had already finished on the phone. "We have to arrange for the reception of the others. Your father's over the border, by the way. They just told me." Tesco addressed his last remark to Ealasaid.

They went out of the library and left me alone. I settled to my task. But first I stood up, and, holding on to the desk, took one more step backwards and then forwards. It was painful.

EIGHTEEN

"I KNOW THAT most of you have had even less time than I to readjust, to read yourselves back into circulation. I must say that you all look remarkably fit for a bunch of ex-convicts." We sat round a faded green-baize table in the dining-room of the house. In better days it had, like the library, been an elegant room. Now it badly needed a coat of paint.

There were twelve of us in all. At least two, and possibly a third, hadn't made it. The attempt at a joke went down badly. Everyone, myself included, was too tense and unsettled to have time for anything but the work in hand. Sir Alexander Mac-Dowall sat on my right; Tesco was on my left. The others in the group included a number of familiar faces: senior civil servants; one or two political figures from my own group and from other ends of the spectrum including Matthews, the ex-Minister of Trade, and Dr Mackinnon, the former leader of the Nationalist extremist group, a man with whom I had never got on politically or socially, but whose dynamism I had admired. At a side-table were Ealasaid, Torrance Junior and three other men who had been doing the work behind the scenes. Round the table we were, with the exception of Tesco, united in having spent the last months in varying degrees of confinement, with the inevitable concentration of minds and singleness of purpose which that forced on us.

"We owe, the country owes, an enormous debt of gratitude to Mr Tesco, Mr Guthrie, Mr Torrance, Miss MacDowall and to our friends Lindsay and MacPake in the States, and to the others who . . ." I started with a formal but genuine expression of appreciation. It was a limp attempt. But everyone echoed it. After some minutes we got down to business.

It seemed to me, and I said so, that as far as our efforts were concerned the main force for change must come from outside.

While we were well served with information by Guthrie and we had the Special Task Unit to call on, any real means of pressing for change from within was totally lacking, as was the possibility of getting our message across about the true state of affairs in the country. Of course people at home knew or guessed a great deal. I had learned that the electorate hadn't entirely acted like sheep; there had been numerous demonstrations, strikes, political rallies, but control by the Bondi Government had been expertly maintained through total censorship of the media. And spreading information by word of mouth is notoriously inaccurate, slow and dangerous.

At Guthrie's suggestion, Tesco had earlier tried to get Whitehall's permission to set up a transmitter from a ship outside territorial waters or beamed in from England. But the former was too difficult and expensive a scheme to launch, and the English Government had refused permission for the latter. We knew they were very much in the picture about what was going on in Scotland, but they were playing it along. Since independence they had taken a lot of trouble to steer clear of following any policies that could be construed as meddling in Scottish internal affairs. And as a frequent critic of English activities in the past I couldn't blame them. The English Broadcasting Corporation were also fairly cautious about putting out news that was too critical of the Bondi Government, so listening in to the English stations would not have given any Scottish listener a full enough picture either. One thing I discovered that the London Government *had* done, however, was to bring in stiff laws on external ownership of firms operating inside England, with the effective object of killing a similar Bondi take-over operation south of the Border.

Our Cabinet in Exile, while it was, hardly surprisingly, not the most effective meeting I have ever chaired, agreed certain courses of action directed at rallying international opinion. We were to wait a few days until we all had had more opportunity of grasping what had been happening and allowing time for cool self-reflection. Then the intention was that I should go

first to London and then to the States to estimate what support
would be forthcoming for our cause. We had to act fast before
the Bondi Government, as we had now come to call them,
were able to get in first. They appeared to have one weakness
which we could exploit to our major advantage. They had
failed, except through their natural and extremely close business
links with the States, to pay much attention to the international
community and to international opinion. A country can only
do that for so long, unless it is exceptionally strong. From the
file of cuttings from the world's press which Tesco had had
collected over the months, criticism of what had been happening in Edinburgh was only too ripe for exploiting. So we made
our deployment. Dr Mackinnon was to go on a flying tour of
Australia and New Zealand to lobby Scottish opinion there;
Matthews was going to Canada for a similar exercise among
the extensive and vociferous Scottish Community there, and I,
I had London and the States. It was a tall order. It was also
expensive, and funds were not large, though MacPake, Lindsay
and the American loyalist group had produced quite a substantial sum of money in a remarkably short space of time. It
remained for us to put it to best advantage.

It was an exhausting week. I was stimulated by the comparative ease with which I took and retained charge of the
operation. We lived and worked in an officers' mess environment at Ravenscliff, sleeping, eating and working on the
premises. There were also a number of young volunteers,
recruited mainly by Guthrie over the past months, who were
there as security guards to help protect us from any attempt by
the Bondi Government to get at us in any way. At that stage,
something in the nature of a real team spirit was created, without the leisure for petty jealousies and rivalries to build up.
There were conflicts of course. But MacDowall helped greatly.
Again I grew to admire his ability to manipulate and control to
the best advantage of all concerned. And, if he helped us all, his
daughter helped me individually. She was my self-appointed

assistant in every way. The communal living helped. I stopped my heavy drinking and began to walk and live again.

London, wet and washed out. The stone of the Government buildings, so recently cleaned, already looked shop-soiled. London hadn't changed much over these past six years; not official London, Whitehall and Westminster. Dark formal suits, a plethora of black umbrellas; how familiar it all was. If anything, the faces of the people were greyer and more strained than I remembered.

It was to be a difficult trip and I was far from clear how I was going to play it or how my arguments might best be brought to bear on this English Government. The English were, after all, committed, as so often in the past, to adopting a role that was, on the face of it, totally passive. Yet behind the scenes, they were working out their destiny with a cold, clear view of where their best interests lay. It would only be with difficulty that I would get their Government to come off the fence and play a more active part in helping to get rid of the Bondi Government. Since they had been subjected to such abuse by us these few years ago when they found that they were no more ruling Great Britain but only little England, their foreign policy had been of the lowest profile, and emulation of the policies of a Sweden or a Switzerland had been the driving force in English political life. After years of welcoming England's adoption of such a stance, I found myself in London to ask it to play the opposite. Apart from everything else, their Foreign Secretary, who would be the moving force behind any Cabinet decisions taken in Downing Street, was the most extreme of the Little Englanders. I didn't have much hope.

We arrived by the night train. Ealasaid MacDowall and Walt Tesco had come with me. Tesco was going on to the States to report back to MacPake and to help pave my way. Using my hotel room as an office, we three spent the morning in rather unsatisfactory meetings with a variety of London/Scottish groups and individuals whom we thought might help. I arranged, not without difficulty, a meeting with their Foreign Secretary for the following afternoon. I presumed at the time that he was reluctant to see me because I now had no status, (and had, if anything, a negative status as an ex-detainee and escaped, publicly-proclaimed corrupt politician) and he was worried about getting protests from the Bondi régime about having received me. But he had another reason for not wanting to meet me as well, as I was to discover. In the end I persuaded him that I had sufficient strings to pull to ensure that there would be even more fuss for him if I were denied an interview.

We had a tiring day, and about seven at night I proposed to the other two that we owed ourselves a break. I suggested a little restaurant I used to go to just off Shaftesbury Avenue. We had a drink at the hotel, summoned a taxi, and went. I took my wheelchair. While I had made a great advance, it was still only a matter of a dozen steps at the most before I was totally exhausted. Ealasaid had booked a corner table. I decided on the spur of the moment to make my own way in. Tesco deposited the folded chair with our coats in the cloakroom and slowly, but upright, I followed them to the table. The fact that I was walking, that I had changed or aged, may have helped to account for the lack of recognition. I could hardly focus across the room, and so stunned was I that I said nothing.

"Are you all right," Ealasaid asked anxiously as I lowered myself into my seat. Tesco pushed my chair in close to the table.

"Rushing things again, that's all," I explained breathlessly. Remembering the sound of a voice heard over a telephone all these months ago, I felt neither angry nor sad; if anything I was elated, even excited. I ordered aperitifis in expansive mood. I was glad I had suggested to Tesco that he come along. At first I had thought of taking Ealasaid out on her own, and Tesco had given me every opportunity to leave him out of the arrangements, but we had been working well as a team and I had felt that those other things could wait. It was doubly fortunate now.

I relaxed. Tesco and Ealasaid must have gathered early on

that my attention wandered. Both had their backs towards the two people at the table on the far side of the room, and I was partly hidden by a lighted candle in its brightly-polished brass holder.

We had finished and were ordering coffee, when I saw the people at the other table preparing to leave. I turned to Tesco.

"If you look casually behind you, there's a man and woman seated by the window on the right. They're on the point of leaving. The man's face; do you know him?"

Tesco eased round carefully in his seat and focused through his pebble lenses.

"Yes, I think so," he said. "I'm not a hundred per cent sure, but I believe it's the man you're seeing tomorrow afternoon. It's their Foreign Secretary, isn't it?"

"I think so too. If we're right, then we're on to something," I said. "You've still got a lot of contacts in the gossip columnist world here, have you?" Tesco nodded.

"Well, plan for a busy night. And what about enlisting a reliable and discreet private detective at this late hour? Can you fix that?"

Again Tesco nodded. "Or I'm quite good at that sort of thing myself," he volunteered. "I've had plenty of practice. I remember once shadowing a well-known film star for hours and finding her . . ."

"Never mind that now." I cut him short. "You've got till tomorrow afternoon. Four o'clock is when I'm meeting that man. Before then I want as much as you can get on him. It could just be vital. Personal and so on. The dirt."

I saw Ealasaid's face crinkle with dislike. "That sort of tactic is hardly your style, Malcolm," she burst out. "In any case why do you think there'll be anything on him important enough for you to use, even if you wanted to? And who's to say if he's the sort that will respond to that sort of thing, other than to kick you out? In any case it's not a very good starting point for dirt-digging, a man and his wife or girl-friend out for a quiet meal."

"That's just the point," I said quietly, shading my head fractionally behind the candlestick. The two people concerned left their table and walked past us to the door. "That's just the point," I repeated. The woman paused beside us for a moment as their overcoats were produced by a waiter. She glanced vacantly in my direction. There was no spark of recognition.

When the English Foreign Secretary had left the restaurant with my wife, I told the others.

As Ealasaid had said the night before, it wasn't my style. But then again it was hardly blackmail—more an irate husband act. And it produced a remarkably favourable response.

NINETEEN

AWAY BELOW, THE undulating evenness of a winter land-
scape; beautiful; always changing, unrecorded because, in
reality, it was the soft subtle tops of the cloud mass viewed
from twenty-three thousand feet. Almost the whole way from
London Heathrow to New York Kennedy Airport, there was
this unbroken, brilliant whiteness. Flying west, the Jumbo
almost kept pace with the sun, so that the day never seemed to
advance or wane. When I wasn't sleeping or eating I was
working on the speech I hoped I should be allowed to make
before the Security Council.

Over Nova Scotia the cloud broke up a little and I had a
glimpse of forests alternating with moss-covered barrenness,
little lakes, flat brown hills and not a trace of man. Then again
it was clear over the coast of Maine with its heavy green intro-
duction to the New England States. Roads appeared, geo-
metrically drawn across the terrain. There was cloud again,
which didn't break up until the spires and towers of Manhattan
appeared to the west. In the gaps, I caught a glimpse of the
Statue of Liberty. As we circled round it I could see the
attractive designs of the oil and other pollution on and in the
water of the Sound.

Arrival at an American port or airport can be either hell or
heaven depending on Customs and Immigration. In recent years
I had been spared the indignity of queueing, being of sufficient
prominence to get the VIP treatment; met by cars at the aircraft, whipped away via discreet VIP lounges, served with
iced drinks and conducted by softly-spoken officials, out
through anonymous side-doors to avoid the batteries of
resident press photographers and reporters. This time I hadn't
expected it. I was now a private citizen, at least in a technical
sense, a former minister of a once independent country.

But the newly-founded Federation of American Caledonian
loyalists had been working hard. And VIPs are selected on two
counts: their intrinsic status, Ambassadors, Kings and the like;
and those whose arrival is likely to cause inconvenience and
upset to the normal smooth running of an airport: actresses,
television stars and people like me with a lot of potential newsworthiness. I didn't know it till I got in, but news of my arrival
and some tantalising hints of the reasons for my visit had leaked
out. So I got the VIP treatment. Only this time they weren't
very good at shielding me from the newsmen. I refused to make
a statement, but there were lots of photographs of me in the
evening editions by the time the driver of the enormous
Cadillac got us along the so-called freeways through the toll-
gates and the hideous traffic jams to the misty impressive sky-
scrapers of central Manhattan.

Five in the afternoon New York time, ten at night London
time; my timing mechanism would take a day or so to readjust.
A hazy series of impressions: MacPake and Lindsay talking to
me non-stop; outside, four constant lanes of slow-moving,
enormous cars; little colour and a lot of dirt, especially when
we hit the city and drove slowly up towards the great glass
wafer of the United Nations building itself.

The Security Council convenes in a much smaller chamber
than the General Assembly. An open circular table is at the
centre, broken at one side; in the middle sit the Secretariat and
the clerks. The Permanent and Temporary Members of the
Council have their seats around the outside. The Delegates'
chairs are of dark blue leather. Behind, four light blue chairs
are for the delegation members. Around, and set high in the
walls on three sides of the Chamber, futuristic glass-fronted
cubicles contain the simultaneous interpreters, the press and
the television men. In tiered seats on the fourth side, sit the
general public. Many seem to have sandwiches and thermos
flasks. As there have been one or two incidents, security guards,
facing away from the Council arena, are much in evidence.

Completing the decoration, a great nineteen-fifties vintage mural is set high behind the Chairman's seat. It depicts the righting of wrongs, men being released from their chains and progressing upwards to freedom, light and happiness. It is as unimpressive as it is dated.

I sat on one side, waiting to be called, wheelchair folded beside me. The English delegate was to propose my being heard, and no dissenting voices were expected. I smiled across at a Dutchman I had known vaguely somewhere in the past, and he beamed warmly back. The Japanese Chairman started calling the meeting to order. Diplomats wandered about in apparently aimless confusion. In the glass boxes, the interpreters adjusted their apparatus. I was surprisingly calm.

Right and left around the table, the skin colouring of the delegates did not always betray the identity of the country they represented. At the United Nations one is plunged into a constant guessing-game, as people stroll about in the lobbies and corridors, and one's hunch is often only resolved for certain when they finally take their seats behind the country labels at the table. Exposure to New York life and the constant international contact at the UN seems to blend the skin pigment to a universal light brown. Perhaps it is my imagination, or perhaps it was the lateness of the hour—seven in the evening here, midnight in London. Or is it just the brightness of the arc lights on the mud-coloured carpet that produces this effect? Dress, equally, is no guide; the Russians, as well or as badly dressed as the Americans in their New England suiting, are just as likely to sport button-down shirts.

Ian Campbell, looking drawn and tired, came into the Chamber. Behind him, and carrying the familiar red despatch box with his papers, walked Guthrie, cold and dark and unchanged. It was a shock to see him there, knowing what I did, but when he glanced briefly in my direction, his look was totally free from any emotion. Behind these two came a number of Campbell's aides. Among them I recognised only de Laski. Campbell, I had discovered from Guthrie, had taken over both of my previous portfolios—home affairs, police, prisons and public order, and also my foreign affairs responsibilities. I also knew from Guthrie that Campbell would be coming to New York. Scotland wasn't a current member of the Security Council, so he, like me, had to sit on the side with his henchmen, until he too would be called.

After much prodding from us and a vast amount of lobbying from Australian and Canadian interests, and particularly precipitated by my personal approach to their Secretary of State in London barely two weeks ago, the English Government had come off their fence and had brought before the Security Council what was listed on the Council Agenda as *The present state of Scotland: a matter of urgent international concern*. Certain Eastern European Countries had backed up this call only too rapidly, conceivably not so much out of any real anxiety about the fate of the former Scottish administration, but because they saw in the debate a further method of hitting, and on this occasion with more than a little justification, at their monster of international capitalism. The Bondi Corporation had strong supporters in Congress, and the United States, for understandable reasons, was adopting a very low profile in the whole affair.

The debate opened in a welter of super-power abuse, only in passing related to Scotland's cause. The delegates spoke rapidly or hesitantly according to their habits, but the slow measured English of the simultaneous translation, on channel two of the six-band system, was always even. I sat listening with the little plastic headphone hooked over my right ear. The translator's voice was perfectly, but not affectedly, cultured, betraying hardly an emotion even when the Russian delegate was belabouring the table and shouting about the imperialist warmongering aims of American big business. A listener on the live Russian channel on the other hand frequently risked his eardrums.

I was involved, so deeply involved in what I had come to do and say. This whole emergency debate was the most important thing in my life for the moment. Yet it was all so low-key. The general air of unemotional *camaraderie* in the Security Council and indeed at the whole United Nations struck me as desperately and shockingly genuine. But it was a very undramatic reflection of the real problems of lives and freedom in ultimate ends of the globe that were being continuously discussed here with impassivity if not with boredom. Delegates might shout and call each other's countries the most unspeakable of names. But, ironically, the genuine hope for the future peace of the world was really demonstrated in the many bars of the UN building afterwards, when angry words were forgotten in the international rounds of drinks. Particularly favoured, I discovered, was that most un-cold-war of drinks—the *Bloody Mary*: basically Russian, intrinsically American.

I put everything into my speech, and flatter myself by thinking it came across well. But it was all a giant charade. I knew as soon as I had finished speaking, as soon as I had seen duplicated copies of what I had said being distributed round the members of the Security Council and seen them set aside with the ever-mounting piles of other speeches, that it was all just words. Everyone had listened, but had not heard. It was part of the game. Emotions, anger, pity, were all rolled out on the stage. One's ability to act these emotions was praised or condemned like reviews in the papers. That was all. My only minor gratification was that Ian Campbell, when called upon to reply, spoke badly, hardly managed to put across his message that the whole debate was an affront, that it was nothing to do with the Security Council and was an internal matter, totally and completely within the competence of the Scottish Government. He had the benefit of speaking to only a handful of members of the Council since the others had walked out in protest. He ended up badly shattered. That hardly mattered either. The Resolution condemning the Bondi Government, when it came, was part of the same game of charades. It had also been tabled by the English, but it was a weak disappointing effort, and only went as far as their Foreign Secretary felt he could get away with in the circumstances, without calling down all our wrath and ill-will on his head. Only when it had been tabled did I see at last the Security Council itself come to life. As part of the game, votes have to be won or lost; the dice are thrown; the various camps and factions conspire and whisper; urgent signs of activity are visible at each delegation, and First Secretaries rush, or rather flit, from delegation to delegation landing at each like flies on a flower or a piece of refuse, to lobby, to cajole, or at least to indulge in the exercise of judging what the likely voting pattern is to be. Some delegations had check-lists on little erasable plastic sheets, registering possible voting intentions: yes; no; doubtful-yes; doubtful-no; amenable to pressure; genuinely undecided, and so on. It comes as a shock to see how the diplomats' game of the world is played.

Waiting for the vote itself, everything subsided to near apathy once more. The relaxed atmosphere, adjusted by the precise coolness of the air-conditioning, began to affect me as well. I watched detachedly as a distinguished East African delegate who had, with pronounced Scots accent denoting his educational background, argued earlier about the evils of neo-colonialism, gradually fell asleep in his chair. It was an understandable attitude. He didn't waken when the vote was announced.

We got a big enough majority in our favour; there were a couple of abstentions, but a veto came from the East Europeans who felt the resolution wasn't couched in strong enough terms. So back to square one. And what did a resolution more or less matter? It wasn't going to solve our problem. MacPake and Lindsay were pleased however. Publicity had its uses, they assured me, and by that time of night I was too tired to argue.

The twenty-third floor of the Waldorf Towers affords a view of little but the uninspiring twenty-third floors of the surrounding blocks. If I wheeled my chair close up to the window I had a limited glimpse of a patch of steaming, lamp-lit street away below, with the occasional late night reveller's car hurtling its way along it.

By nature, I am not an extravagant person and I had protested at being put up at the Waldorf. But my backers, every one of whom seemed overly public-relations-conscious, had insisted that I should, and that was an end to it. They even paid for Tesco to have the adjoining room. The Treasury never allowed any of us to stay there when I was a Minister.

My room was spacious and well furnished in a would-be eighteenth-century French style. On my bedside table was a Gideon Bible and a copy of Conrad Hilton's *Be my guest*. For the price, who wouldn't?

I wheeled myself through to the bathroom, an equally magnificent tiled affair, and I admit to having been impressed by the three taps, hot, cold, and ice-cold water. The Hilton service ran to having a chromium-plated rack specially fitted to the bath to allow invalids like me to manipulate themselves in and out of the water. I took advantage of the bath and rack and then rolled into bed.

I was too tired. It was late even by New York time and I was five hours ahead. It would soon be dawn in Edinburgh. Yet I was tense and couldn't sleep and I turned on the light again and lay in bed watching American television for the first time for years. For twenty-four hours a day, year in and year out, a constant cycle of old movies and late late shows interspersed at ridiculously short intervals with ridiculously long commercials, is churned out on numerous channels for the transatlantic insomniac. The westerns and B-features were soporific, and after about half an hour I was about to switch off with the assistance of the remote control panel, when I heard a slight sound and noticed the gilt door-handle of my room turning slowly.

I had never locked doors since my injury. I felt I would rather be robbed than risk creating barriers should I need urgent help. I have always suffered slightly from claustrophobia and my lack of mobility heightened this anxiety in me. But the thought flashed through my mind that I should have been more careful in New York; one heard so many stories of what violence there was round every corner. Yet I had a telephone and a bell after all, and this was the Waldorf.

Guthrie slipped silently into the room. He was wearing a blue silk dressing-gown, but I noticed that he was fully dressed underneath. He barely apologised.

"It seemed too good an opportunity to miss," he began, his dark face crushed into something like a smile. We shook hands.

"We're on the twentieth floor and there's a staircase round the corner from my room. The Waldorf's a funny place," he went on, as if he'd spent his life in the place. "Especially during the United Nations General Assembly, every room is taken by delegations of Ministers and diplomats from every country under the sun. It's so remarkably anonymous. Jews meet Arabs here, Chinese meet Russians, Russians meet Americans and the CIA reputedly employs three-quarters of the chamber-maids."

As Guthrie finished speaking, the room door was flung open again and Tesco, with remarkable agility, was up close behind him. To my startled interest he seemed to have a gun in his hand. Then he recognised Guthrie.

"Sorry," Tesco said. "We can't be too careful. You might have been one of Campbell's men."

We all laughed nervously. I realised once more what a versatile man Tesco was, and that I was being well looked after. I would have to ask him where he got the gun.

"It's good to see you," I said, "and I mean it. You are doing a great job."

"It's only the beginning." Guthrie looked bitterly serious. "But I see the odd glimpse of light."

"No one saw you coming?"

"Except for Mr Tesco here, they're all sound asleep. Campbell with nervous exhaustion, and de Laski's got a man-eating whore with him."

I had forgotten the television. A religious programme had come on; a bishop was talking with a blues singer. It appeared to be a live show and I wondered at their dedication at that time of night. I reached over to press the off button, but Tesco stopped me.

"It's what's known in the spy trade as audio cover, isn't it, Mr Tesco?" Guthrie grinned. He seemed to be enjoying things. I had never seen him like this before. He was a much more confident individual than the man who had quietly and efficiently run my life as my Private Secretary. It's a trap Ministers too frequently fall into, treating and accepting their officials as efficient, characterless automata. Yet ninety-nine times out of a hundred the nominal political boss is surrounded by men not only of infinitely superior intellect but also with wider attitudes to life.

I started to question Guthrie through my tiredness. I was aware of myself talking as if viewing the situation from a great distance. He cut me short.

"There's no time. I must get back. I came only to give you this." He handed me a large sealed envelope.

"What is it?"

"It's a blueprint. In a way it's an extension of my doctoral thesis at the Harvard Business School. But you'll find it's not just theoretical background; it's a whole plan of campaign."

I started to open the envelope, but he told me to leave it till the morning. "It's very complex, Minister," he said. "Keep it safe. Perhaps as he has a gun, Mr Tesco could look after it for you. It could be dynamite if we light the blue touchpaper in the right place and at the right time."

It was after they both had left the room and I had turned out the light at last, that I realised Guthrie had addressed me as *Minister*.

TWENTY

AT RAVENSCLIFF, NERVES were beginning to fray. It had been too long with nothing to show for it. This morning's meeting had been a disaster and it had been much my fault. Dr Mackinnon had come out with one platitude too many: something about not giving up one bondage in exchange for another without a fight. I had made a disparaging remark, and Mackinnon had retaliated with a stream of invective directed at my leadership of which I remember little except his last remark: "How could anyone take a man with a name like Mockingham seriously?" He had walked out. I had to laugh, and most of the others did too, but it was a measure of the petty levels to which we had sunk. I made it up with Mackinnon afterwards, but things couldn't last. We needed action.

It was two weeks since the Security Council debate. And what had been achieved in the meantime? Precious little. A group of intellectually active middle-aged men, separated from our previous lives and present families, living in some considerable discomfort in a large and increasingly seedy country house miles from anywhere. It was symbolic that a growing amount of time was now spent in simple self-administration. At times I felt Ravenscliff was rather more like a monastery than an officers' mess, and indeed Matthews had started planting a little plot of garden with lettuce seed, as if he fully expected to harvest the crop.

We had little in common except our aim and our prison-graduate experience. We were getting on each other's nerves, we had no success to speak of, and, more dangerously, there were signs of definite mistrust growing up as we became aware of how many of our former colleagues had been bought over by Bondi. Some who had been, like us, arrested, were now free, active and reinstated again. We could only presume they had accepted what had been offered them. And if it could happen to them, might it not happen, might it not come about that some of us be tempted by the prospect of returning to a life of near normality? The calls of my colleagues' families alone were all-pervading. Even MacDowall and his daughter were worried. They knew Lady MacDowall was comfortable enough since messages had been smuggled to and fro, but it couldn't dispel their worries. It was something even I tried to understand. People had had enough.

Action, action. We had international support. But that was meaningless in real terms. We were civilised men and assassination was hardly in our line even if we had had the means. Support for us in Scotland was also in doubt, since many of our names, like mine, had been efficiently discredited in the public view, for fraud and corruption. We were hardly likely to be welcomed as honest men, particularly in an increasingly totalitarian environment where the media were so strictly controlled. We got the Scottish papers and when our names appeared at all it was to ridicule rather than attack: much the best psychological weapon. If we thought of ourselves as a sort of Government in Exile, we were described rather as a bunch of high-grade criminals on the run from justice. Foreign public opinion, the results of such things as the Security Council debate, when they were reported at all, were presented in Scotland in the most biased light imaginable. We used to sit complaining at how people could be so gullible as to believe all this, without appreciating the first rule of State control: that lies are sanctified by constant repetition.

We drew up a list of prime targets. There were twenty-four names on it: the Bondi Cabinet, the Police Commissioner, the new Governor of the Reserve Bank and so on. Of these, when they were examined in more depth, nearly half were imports, Bondi-men through and through, most of them, at a guess, with American passports in their pockets. But that left quite a few people to deal with, and we were not so naïve as to believe that the removal of these would be the end of it. The whole superstructure of the new State was well slotted in behind them. A counter-*coup*, the use of force, was hopelessly out of the question, but how else could one get to the root of the problem?

It was late afternoon. The rain had slackened to a fine drizzle and Ealasaid and I decided on a short walk. When I say that, I mean that she did the walking, pushing me in my wheelchair. The ground was too rough for me to attempt to walk, and besides, I had been doing too much exercising of late, and a specialist whom I had called in, in the enforced absence of Professor Taller, had advised me strongly against doing too much too soon. My thigh and calf muscles ached unbearably at times.

We went down the long drive and turned off through what had once been the walled garden. It was now hopelessly overgrown; only one corner of it was cultivated with a row or two of rather worm-eaten spring cabbage-seedlings put in by the old man who passed for gardener. It compared badly with the neatness and order which had greeted me when I was abducted to the Bondi country headquarters these few months ago.

From the far end of the garden, a path led along by the river. The trees were coming into leaf, and the rain gave everything a pleasant refreshed smell. Ealasaid and I talked business. Once or twice recently I had tried to be really informal, tried to get back to the ease of our conversations when we had first met. But she appeared hesitant, as if holding something back. I didn't press her.

"Don't you ever feel like giving up?" she asked suddenly. I half turned in my chair to glance up at her. She looked seriously at me. "All these people, you, me. What are we all doing here? Don't you feel it's so unreal?"

"Too often."

"How long are we going to go on? We're all beginning to feel the strain. It was all right at first, for you all. You found this place such a welcome freedom. But now? I see the frustration working even on my father. For one thing, he hasn't enough to do and he worries about my mother. Planning and so on is all very well, but there's nothing for him, for any of us, to get our teeth into. Isn't it time to call it off?"

"Don't I know it," I muttered. "But what good does it do going around . . ." I paused. It was revealing that I could find even her irritating now.

"Sorry. It's so obvious. I shouldn't have said it," she responded.

"It needed saying." I lapsed into silence for a moment. She was right. Of course she was right. We were playing silly games, trying to be the Government in Exile, when we should be back home picking up the bits and making peace with those in power. Wasn't it just jealousy after all? They'd got us out, and we were jealous of our former power. Was there really all that much more to it? Not all that many people inside the country had been protesting about the change of régime. Why should we? Were the workers any worse off? Were there fewer strikes or more unemployment than there had been when I had been a Minister? The figures certainly didn't show it, though they could have been rigged. Weren't our opinions too remote and subjective? If the people didn't mind what sort of government they had, why should we lose sleep over it? Why not do as others had done: go back and make peace with Ian Campbell and his crew? *Campbell*: the name stuck in my gullet.

Ealasaid noticed my lapse into gloomy mood and changed the subject. "It's a pity you can't get up there yet, up to the hill behind the house over there," she said. "That's where the river comes from. I walked right over the top when we first arrived. It was an extremely cold day, and there was a hard frost. It was beautiful. I found a spring which feeds the river, near a little lake, high up, just below the summit. The water had forced its way through the ground, and frozen into gorgeous shapes." She stopped and I applied the handbrake on my chair. "Later," she said, "I'll take you up and show you where it comes from. When you're back on your feet again."

She smiled down at me, and I smiled back. I felt very happy.

We stayed motionless for some moments, then something she had said cut through my thoughts. "Where it comes from . . . Of course . . . How stupid." My smile turned rapidly to an idiotic grin, and I began to laugh. Ealasaid looked down oddly at me.

"Perhaps we'd better be getting back," she said anxiously.

"No, wait. Listen to me," I replied. "I'm going to give them action."

I had briefly skimmed through Guthrie's *blueprint* on the plane home from New York and then had handed it back to Tesco saying that we would think about it later. I hadn't actually dismissed his idea; it was just that it seemed so impractical in the circumstances. In any case we were returning to Ravenscliff flushed with the dubious victory of the Security Council debate behind us, full of convinced beliefs of how easy it was going to be to convert the nation back to a democratic path. It was only now, two weeks later, with the cold realities of trying to unseat the Bondi Government so effectively thrust in our faces, that Guthrie's idea of hitting at the source came properly to life. All I had done was to waste two valuable weeks.

It would be far from easy, but at least it offered the chance of real action which the other sort of plotting failed to do. My enthusiasm after the walk with Ealasaid carried me through to the meeting I called as soon as we returned to the house. In the end it was sufficiently genuine to carry the others with it. They had their doubts in plenty, but we all would have them at various stages in the preparation of the plan.

It started badly. They sat round the big table in the library waiting for me to explain. I began by apologising that I hadn't worked things out in detail. Guthrie had done some sterling groundwork, but careful planning and the greatest secrecy would be needed if there was to be any hope of success. I put Guthrie's argument at length.

"We've been agreed over and over again during the past months about the difficulties of converting the political opinions of the public. We've agreed also that while force—a *coup*—might work, it is totally impractical; in sum, we couldn't hope to change the *status quo*. But the stupidity of it is that we've been looking too hard at the end-product, the Bondi Government itself."

I stared fiercely round at my colleagues. They stared blankly back. I caught Dr Mackinnon stifling a yawn, and wondered for a moment whether I was thinking and talking nonsense.

"We've got to get at the source," I said triumphantly. Again there were blank faces. Only in Sir Alexander MacDowall's expression did I trace a note of quickening interest. "It's difficult to create a meaningful run of confidence against a government unless things are very bad indeed. But it's been proved to be only too easy to create a crisis of confidence in the business world, and that's what we're going to do with the Bondi Corporation."

"But it's a multi-million dollar consortium. As safe as houses," Mackinnon grunted. The majority in the room seemed to agree with him.

"That's true. And it will probably remain generally true. But what we have to concoct, what we're going to try to do, is to create at least a short-term slump in its business respectability. The Stock Markets in London and Wall Street will do the rest for us."

Mackinnon snorted, stood up and went and stared out of the window. I levered myself to my feet. While I had no longer been keeping it a close secret, many of them hadn't seen me standing before. It helped gain their attention. "While I remain in charge we're going to try." I glared round the room. There was silence. I wasn't sure how they were going to take it. Out of the corner of my eye I saw MacDowall move as if to speak. Then he stopped. Dr Mackinnon had turned in the window. He was facing me.

"Very well, let's hear about it," he said. "It's a chance. Perhaps it's the only one."

I lowered myself thankfully back into my chair.

We planned it like a military operation. Over the next weeks, lists of every major city editor and economic correspondent of the top dozen newspapers in the States and in Europe were drawn up. We went to great lengths to prepare the ground with reliable business consultants, brokers and investment directors. We put MacPake and the American loyalist men on to similar lines of enquiry in the States. In a matter of three weeks, working from Guthrie's blueprint, we had as complete a picture as possible of the whole Bondi set-up, right down to detailed charts of their company organisation, which we pinned up on the library walls. We allotted ourselves sectors of the organisation, investigating their trading and investment patterns in as much depth as we could from the available material.

D-day was to be Monday, 2nd May. Three days before then, Matthews and two of the others flew to New York. Mackinnon left the next day for Basle, and Sir Alexander MacDowall went to cover Frankfurt and Dusseldorf. They all had their lists of contacts. They all set themselves up with the only equipment they were going to need: a timetable and a telephone. At Ravenscliff, we waited.

The effectiveness of the story was its simplicity. At the pre-arranged time the telephoning began: the Bondi Corporation was insolvent; bankrupt. Severe mismanagement was the cause.

The rumours spread at once. We started up in each country as the Stock Markets opened. But rumours aren't quite enough for cautious stockbrokers and wary city editors. They are as used as racing tipsters to deliberate planting of false information. They queried the story and the evidence. The evidence, equally carefully fabricated, was produced for the asking. Then the geographical scale of our misinformation effort began to pay dividends. "If you don't believe me," the incredulous brokers and journalists in London were told, check up with your colleagues, your business contacts in Wall Street, among the gnomes of Zurich or Basle or Frankfurt or on the Paris Bourse. Through MacPake, the Americans had even placed a man in Tokyo. It was almost conclusive. Their colleagues and contacts had the same story, and the same evidence. It was too much. Big crashes had happened before and it was safer to stand right clear. And where the public puts up with a lot of rumour before even thinking of changing their political loyalties, when it comes to their pockets, their investments, their profits and their dividends it's a very different matter.

It was frighteningly successful. Within hours, millions had been lopped off the value of Bondi Shares in the world's Stock Markets. Share prices plummetted. Naturally, the Bondi directors came in with a rapid statement vehemently denying the rumour. But Boards of Directors usually issue such statements whether the facts fit or not. In this case they could well have won some credence with their protestations of complete solvency, but we were ready for this and prepared with our second wave of rumours. This time the story was that the Bondi directors' statement was a cover-up for even more serious deficiences in the viability of the Corporation. We leaked detailed background about interlocking Bondi affiliates to city editors and to leading stockbroking firms. Sufficient fact was employed to give weight to the elements of fiction. It was put across anonymously or in the strictest confidence, and that added to its newsworthiness. Record drops were recorded on Wall Street and in the City of London.

At stage three we fed in the Scottish aspect. The story was linked to the world's condemnation of the Bondi Government in the Security Council debate. And that, to hard-headed speculators on the Exchanges, was complete, undeniable fact. Press releases, carefully backed up with confidential briefings of selected journalists, were fed into the complex. It was all systems go. Political scandal grew out of and fed on the more effective commercial scandal. The former justified the latter. Reports from Basle, Frankfurt and Paris came whistling across the wires that the seeds of the Bondi collapse—the biggest multi-national consortium to go down since the Great Crash of 1929, so the headlines had it—had been planted when it over-stretched itself by taking over Scotland.

On the basis of even such well-prepared rumour, however, we knew only too well that commercial collapse could not be forced through to the end. The Bondi Corporation was, as far as we knew, basically sound, and it would only be a matter of time till their directors got on top of the panic. They might even make out of it. We had to act fast on the home front.

The process was self-generating. Wednesday, 4th May, about ten in the morning, and a large black Chevrolet pulled up the Ravenscliff drive and stopped at the main door. Apart from the uniformed chauffeur, there was only one person in it: Dobbs, the man who had abducted me.

Ealasaid met him at the door, he gave his name and straight-away demanded to see me. He hurriedly followed this up by announcing that he hadn't come on his own behalf; that he had a personal message for me from Ian Campbell, as if such an explanation would prove *entrée* enough. I refused to see him at first and said that if there was a message, it could be left in writing. After some minutes, Ealasaid returned and told me that he was refusing to be put off, however, and a mixture of this, her arguments and my own curiosity, persuaded me to let him be shown in.

If I had expected him to be in any way abashed or embar-rassed at renewing our acquaintanceship, I was disappointed. He came in looking as bloated but as morosely correct as I had remembered him. I noticed a slight fluttering of his right hand as he wondered whether, if he offered to shake hands, I would refuse. Wisely he decided on caution. I stayed seated, looking up coldly as he approached my desk.

"I've been asked to bring you a message from the Minister."
It was a bad beginning, and Dobbs realised it at once. "From
Mr Campbell," he corrected himself.

"Then let me have it."

"It's a verbal message. Strictly for your ears alone." Dobbs
turned slightly and looked at Ealasaid who made as if to
leave.

"No. Stay here please, Miss MacDowall. Now, Mr Dobbs,
would you mind saying what you have to say? We have a great
deal of work in hand, as you will realise."

Dobbs's eyes flickered uneasily as he wondered whether to
take a seat. In the end he remained standing.

"He would like to meet you."

"I live and work here. He knows where to find me."

"It would be very difficult for him to come south of the
Border at the present time."

"That's his misfortune." I was becoming increasingly
impatient and irritated by my former stand-in Private Secretary's manner.

"He wants to put a proposition to you. He guarantees that if
you come to Edinburgh to meet him you will be unharmed.
There will be no attempt to detain you."

"In that case, he should have sent an emissary in whom I
could have had confidence, particularly on the subject of
detention."

Dobbs flushed, hesitated momentarily and went on: "He
would like you to come back and join him; rejoin his Government. He'd like you to come up and meet him to discuss the
terms."

For a few moments I was totally nonplussed by the unbelievable nature of Dobbs's message. "I understood there was still
nominally a Prime Minister," I replied slowly. "Campbell's
title surely is still just Minister of Home Affairs. In any case I
have to assume that it's the Bondi Government who've issued
the invitation." I pivoted my wheelchair round and away from
the desk. Outside the window, I could see Dobbs's chauffeur

painstakingly cleaning some mud off the Chevrolet. I turned back to face him and, as I did so, I caught sight of Ealasaid out of the corner of my eye. She was sitting in the far corner of the room, watching us intently.

"That's the point. The Minister, Mr Campbell, wants your help. He said to tell you, persuade you that it's all got out of hand. The PM's totally out of things. He's a cypher and he's aged enormously in recent months. But you must have known that. You must surely know too that Mr Campbell's not a free agent, and that the Bondi directors, Carlyle, de Laski and the others—they're running everything. They've got some hold over him and Mr Campbell wants to break that hold, get back to the beginning again."

"Are you suggesting that Campbell didn't know what he was doing, Dobbs? Are you?" I repeated fiercely. "Don't waste my time any further if that's all you've got to say. You . . . he . . . the lot of you went into it with your eyes open, and came out with your wallets bulging. Now it's going wrong and you're rushing for cover." I was furious. The insolent nerve of the man left me almost speechless.

"I've come to offer you, on my Minister's behalf, free passage back and a Cabinet seat . . ." Dobbs repeated woodenly.

I suddenly knew that I couldn't put up with much more, that I would be forced to hit the man if he stayed.

"Get out, Dobbs," I hissed. "Get out before I bloody . . ." I pressed hard on the arms of my wheelchair and pushed myself till I knew I could have stood upright. My knuckles were white. But something held me back, and I remained seated. Dobbs stared at me almost as if afraid.

There was a moment or two's silence, then, "*Get out*," I shouted. I saw Ealasaid stand up and come forward as if to restrain me. I ignored her.

"Mr Guthrie said . . ." Dobbs was pale now. His podgy frame shook.

I stared back at him and a glimpse of the uncertainty he had caused must have shown through, because he immediately gained in confidence. "He told me to say that it was most important."

"What Guthrie may or may not have said is of absolutely no interest or concern to me," I said deliberately. I hoped I didn't show any trace of enthusiasm, but perhaps I responded a fraction too quickly to sound genuine. Dobbs saw a further opening and took it.

"He said to tell you that he supported the Minister's request. You would understand, he said."

I was in an immediate dilemma. I must on no account give Dobbs any suggestion that Guthrie was anything more to me than a turncoat Private Secretary. But on the other hand I was well aware that the message meant either that Dobbs was sincere or . . . or that Guthrie had been found out and that his name was being used for some reason not yet apparent to me.

There was nothing I could do. I couldn't trust myself to respond further without giving my confusion away, so on an impulse, I moved the wheels of my chair counter to each other, turning my back on Dobbs. "Get out," I said softly once more.

I watched his reflection in the window. I saw him wait for a moment, confused by my reaction. Then he shrugged as if to himself, turned on his heel and swiftly left the room.

Tesco came in and joined us immediately Dobbs had left.

"I was listening outside," he explained. "Quite a development."

"I don't believe a word of it," I said abruptly. "Though I must admit Dobbs throwing in Guthrie's name caught me off balance."

"What does it mean?" Ealasaid asked.

"I think I have the answer." Tesco sounded as if he were about to come up trumps. "See what young Torrance has just delivered from Edinburgh." He handed me over a bundle of sheets of smudged and inaccurate typescript.

"It's from Special Task Unit," he said. "They've got back on target again. It's taken them some time, but they're working against terrible odds up there, not being able to work through the telephone people as they used to." He sat back anxiously in an armchair, produced a packet of battered cigarettes and lit one.

"I've never seen you smoke before, Walt," I said irrelevantly. Tesco frowned and said nothing. Then I began to read.

The niceties of editing were left to the reader as time had been the all-important essential, but after the first page I understood Tesco's worried look. It was a transcript of three men talking. One was Campbell; his interlocutors, as became clear, were de Laski and Carlyle.

CAMPBELL: You wanted to see me?

DE LASKI: Sit down, Campbell. There's not much time.

CAMPBELL: I've heard about the rumours on Wall Street and the City. Is it true what they're saying?

DE LASKI: Of course it's not true, you fool.

CAMPBELL: All right, all right, there's no need to be abusive. I was only asking. What are you doing about it?

DE LASKI: We can probably cope. But it caught us on the hop. Whoever's been doing it knows far too much. Our guess is that Mockingham and MacDowall are behind it, but they must be getting their information from somewhere. Have you any ideas about that?

There was a pause

CAMPBELL: No. No, why should I? I'm only dealing with the political side. You're the business experts. You know I don't have that sort of brain. . . . What are you suggesting?

DE LASKI: Don't get so worked up, Campbell, or Carlyle and I might think you've got a guilty conscience.

CAMPBELL: I don't know what you're talking about.

DE LASKI: Your Private Secretary . . .

CAMPBELL: Dobbs?

DE LASKI: No; the other one.

CAMPBELL: Oh yes. Guthrie. He's very efficient.

DE LASKI: He sees everything you do?

CAMPBELL: Of course. That's his job. He's much more with it than Dobbs, you know.

DE LASKI: As I suspected. And so whether you understand all the papers about the Bondi Corporation that come your way or whether you don't, Guthrie might?

CAMPBELL: Oh come now. What are you suggesting? Guthrie's very good you know.

DE LASKI: Guthrie was seen coming out of Mockingham's room at the Waldorf in New York. It was the middle of the night, Campbell. Doesn't that strike even you as being a bit odd?

Again there was a pause

CAMPBELL: It's like that is it?

DE LASKI: It's like that, Campbell. Now what are you going to do about it?

CAMPBELL: What am I going to . . . ? But, but you must be able to think of something. You're in it too. Tell me what you want. I'll . . .

DE LASKI: Let me explain it to you slowly, Campbell, in businessmen's terms. Now when an organisation the size of the Bondi Corporation gets hammered about the Stock Markets of the world, something's got to give; something's got to go.

CAMPBELL: But you're an enormous multi-national, as safe as . . . as safe as . . .

DE LASKI: Financially perhaps, and even that's a bit tricky, I hear; but politically we're not safe at all. That UN Security Council fiasco where you, Campbell, *you*, played your hand so badly, has let us in for a lot of trouble. Confidence in us has gone, and to top it all, the State Department are at last beginning to get all anxious. I wondered when that would happen. It was all right so long as there was no fuss and

America wan't directly involved, but now lobbies are forming and so on. It's all right if it's the CIA working in some developing country to keep the Commies out and puppets like you in power, but this is different. The Bondi Directors back in Dallas are worried about a Congressional Enquiry. And d'you know what that means, Campbell? It means a whole lot more trouble.

There was a further pause

CAMPBELL: But what must I do? (*Pause*) *Oh my God.*

DE LASKI: Quite simple. You've got to get a democratic government going again; one above any suspicion, clean, above-board and internationally respectable. That's all. We're going to lie low for a bit. You're obviously going to have to see who you can get to join you, as your name is mud, Campbell. Call it a Government of National Reconstruction if you like. In fact that's quite a good idea. Think about it. You have a couple of minutes.

Pause

CAMPBELL: And if I can't?

DE LASKI: Then it's quite simple, Campbell. We cut our losses, Bondi pulls out and leaves you to the wolves.

The transcriber had noted on the typescript that Campbell had broken down at this point. After a few minutes in which drinks were produced, the conversation continued

CAMPBELL: I'll get Mockingham. He'll come back.

DE LASKI: You think so? I don't.

CAMPBELL: I'll try.

DE LASKI: There's very little time.

CAMPBELL: What about Guthrie?

DE LASKI: That's another matter. That affects Bondi Corporation security. I think we must . . .

There the transcript ended.

"What happened?" I asked Tesco softly.

"Someone in the Op's room pulled the wrong switch. Human error. They're very sorry."

TWENTY-ONE

IT WAS A unique sensation coming at last over the crest of
Soutra and seeing the familiar grey haze of Edinburgh spread
away to the North, the black shape of Arthur's Seat and
Salisbury Crags rising clear above the morning mist. It was an
emotional moment for us and we were all excited in an anxious,
tense way. We had no real idea of what to expect.

Tesco drove, Ealasaid beside him in the front, and I sat with
MacDowall in the back. I had objected to her coming, but she
had insisted, and in the end her father had given in. We reached
Edinburgh in under three hours of fast driving, the only stops a
brief one for customs clearance at the Border and in Jedburgh
to buy the morning's *Scotsman*. I glanced through the paper and
thought I detected the signs of censorship slipping away. For
the first time since I had been released and had access to newspapers again, the main editorial was critical of the Government. The front page splashed a headline about trade union
fears of the massive unemployment that the potential collapse
of the vast Bondi industrial network would bring in its
wake.

Our decision hadn't been reached without hours of argument
and discussion; in the end none of us was sure that we were
doing the right thing. But the prospect of action proved a
stronger case than the uncertainty promised by continuing to
delay at Ravenscliff. So we were coming back, I and my
advisers, determined to bring things to a head one way or
another. There were a variety of reasons. I had no intention of
responding to Campbell's request, but after the situation
revealed by the intercepted conversation, and with the news
that the Bondi people were planning to lie low for a bit, I was
coming back to play them at their own game. I was now prepared to take the risks involved in pretending to go along with

Campbell's offer and then using my position to try and break him. I am not a vindictive or sadistic man, but I wanted to do that. The news that the State Department were getting anxious and that there was the prospect of a Congressional Enquiry, offered further possibilities of wrecking the Bondi Government. And quite apart from anything else, Guthrie had to be warned that they were on to him, if it wasn't too late already. Speed was essential.

We drove through the outskirts, down past the University, then turned left up the High Street to the New National Assembly Building at the top of The Mound. I estimated I'd find Campbell in his office there at this time of day. In through the gates, across the forecourt, Tesco pulled up with too much of a flourish at the main door. I recognised through the car window the familiar faces of two of the beribboned National Assembly ushers as they came out of the huge plate-glass doors and looked towards us. As Tesco and MacDowall struggled to erect my wheelchair and transfer me into it, they came across curiously, perhaps to help, perhaps to question our presence in a restricted area. Then they recognised me. I saw shock spread across one elderly military face after the other. They focused on MacDowall in turn and slowly one of them raised his right hand in a smart salute. A moment's hesitation and the other followed suit.

"Good morning, Sir, Mr Mockingham, Sir," one of them breathed. He was ashen-faced. His consternation had the effect of steadying my nerves, and I smiled a distant friendly greeting as if yesterday had been the last time.

The same man summoned up courage and asked nervously: "Can I help you, Sir, or you, Sir Alexander, Sir?" The "Sirs" tripped over each other in his desire to say the right thing.

"We've come to see Mr Campbell," I said shortly. "I hope he's here."

"Oh, yes, Sir, he is. He's been here all night. He's very busy these days. Is he expecting you, Sir?"

I ignored the question.

"Shall I go and warn . . . tell him." The usher made to go back towards the building. His colleague hovered uncertainly beside him.

"No."

"I beg your pardon, Sir?"

"No," I repeated. "I'll need your help to lift me and my chair up the steps." I didn't want any more advance warning given than was strictly necessary.

Up the steps, through the familiar tiled central lobby to the lifts and up to the first floor. The whole place was deserted. Along the rather austere corridors to what had been my office. A nail stuck out of the wall beside the door where a portrait of me had once hung.

MacDowall marched in front and flung open the door of the outer office. Dobbs stood up shakily as I wheeled myself in. Tesco and Ealasaid walked with the two ushers close behind.

"Tell him we're here," I ordered. Dobbs catapulted himself towards the double doors that connected the outer office and Campbell's room and opened them wide. Before he had time to speak I wheeled myself violently forward and he had to jump out of the way to avoid being hit by my chair.

"Good morning, Campbell," I said.

He stood up behind the great rosewood desk where he had been working. Behind him, the long windows looked out magnificently over the city as it sparkled in the clear May sun. Campbell looked pale and drawn, but, at a guess he had been that already, and it camouflaged any feeling of shock he felt at our arrival.

"I'm glad you've come after all," he said after a moment. He walked unsteadily round the side of the desk and came towards me. He stretched out his hand in greeting and I ignored it. He hesitated, turned and said:

"Good morning, Sir Alexander."

MacDowall, grey, half-moon spectacles perched as always

mid-way down his nose, moved his head in a slight movement of acknowledgement, but said nothing.

"Will you sit down, gentlemen. Er . . . Miss MacDowall I presume, and Mr . . ."

I noticed that Dobbs had disappeared, presumably to call reinforcements. We remained in a sort of semi-circle facing Campbell. He was visibly shaken. For a moment I felt sorry for him and was about to say something to get things moving when it all came tumbling out of him in a frightening crescendo of hysteria.

"I'm in a mess. A mess . . . It's dreadful. They've got me completely tied up and I can't move a finger without their permission. I need your help. We can get rid of them together, Mockingham. You and I can get rid of them. De Laski and Carlyle got me into this. They blackmailed me. It was a little financial indiscretion that happened years ago, but they're expert at getting me to compound my fault. You must believe me. *You must believe me.*" He shouted the words.

I cut him short. "Where are they now?"

"Who? . . . Carlyle . . . de Laski?"

"Yes."

"They're leaving for the States, for Dallas, this morning. There's an emergency Board meeting. They're trying to work out what to do next. You've got them worried. They won't be back for at least three days, Mockingham. We can get it all fixed before they come back. You and me, Mockingham. We can ban them coming back into the country. We can . . ."

Campbell was standing facing us. We had our backs to the door. We watched him dry up in horror. I half turned in my chair as de Laski and Carlyle followed by Dobbs and Guthrie came into the room. Guthrie was slightly to the fore; Dobbs held a pistol trained at his back.

"Good morning, Mr Mockingham. *Goodness.* Sir Alexander, Miss MacDowall, and you must be Mr Tesco. Well, well. That *is* an unexpected bonus." De Laski took his pipe out of his mouth and beamed as he walked slowly into the very centre of the room.

An hour later, and we sat as if in committee: MacDowall, Ealasaid, Tesco and I down one side of the table; de Laski, Carlyle, Campbell and Dobbs on the other. Only Guthrie seemed to be displaced at one end. Dobbs's gun had disappeared, but there were two uniformed American Security men at ease by the door, and we had been warned there were more outside.

De Laski, who gave no sign if he knew that Campbell had been in the middle of trying to ditch his Bondi links, started by informing us baldly that they had caught Torrance's son on return from his latest trip to Ravenscliff. They had been watching out for him for some days after checking out all Guthrie's contacts. He had still had a copy of the transcript of the conversation with him. That had been more than careless.

"We couldn't have planned it better," de Laski said. "You knew what we were intending; you came of your own free will. You'll now have to stay here willingly or unwillingly and we'll have to think again. You see, we were about to report back to the Directors in Dallas—not quite in disgrace, you understand, but they weren't, strictly speaking, pleased. Whatever happens, now that we have you here, we have the means to show that as far as the world is concerned, the Government is about to go all democratic once again. How does taking on the portfolio of Minister of Home Affairs again grab you, Mr Mockingham?" de Laski smiled, charm written all over his face. "Just a titular position, you understand. You give us your name to use for the outward presentation, we do the work. I guess our geriatric of a Prime Minister will hardly notice."

"What the hell d'you mean?" whimpered Campbell plaintively.

"Shut up, Campbell. We'll make you Minister of Public Works or something," de Laski barked sarcastically. "Oh, in addition, Mr Mockingham, you'll be calling off your campaign. I must congratulate you on trying to break the Bondi Corporation. Not that I think you would have succeeded in the end."

"You seemed to be saying otherwise in the transcript, when you were bullying Campbell," I said. Then, as I saw no harm in trying to keep the division in their ranks going, I came in with the revelation that Campbell had been attempting to do a deal with me before they had arrived back. Campbell turned white with fear and started bleating that it was all lies, but de Laski merely shrugged, dismissed it with remarkable *sang froid*, and with no trace of surprise.

"You must remember, Mr Mockingham, Carlyle and I are businessmen. Campbell here, like you, is a would-be politician, though I give you he's hardly in the same league. But neither of you has a binding need to keep your faith. Politics, like diplomacy, is the art of deception, and you're only answerable for your lies to a gullible electorate at five-year intervals. It's all I would expect of Campbell. We, on the other hand, have to answer in precise monetary and material terms to our Board of Directors and through them to the shareholders. We're not in the game on our own account, except indirectly through our pursuit of the Bondi Corporation's welfare. We're paid by results."

"Anything goes under that excuse." I felt more amused than angry at de Laski's far-fetched description of the business world's honesty and integrity.

"Doing one's duty to the State, just as to one's employer, can justify a great deal," I went on. "It can provide a reason, but it can't excuse. The Nazi soldier was only secondly fighting for himself. First came the Fatherland. For you it's the Bondi Corporation. There's no difference."

"Oh come now, Mr Mockingham, you're dramatising things again. But you're right in one way. Means and methods to me are justified by the ends. This time the choice, the end, is simpler, and more extreme. You join us, give us your support to create our picture of democracy, or the alternative cannot again be house arrest. We cannot, you understand, let you loose or risk you escaping a second time. Once was careless; a second error would meet with a severe reprimand from the Bondi Board. Carlyle and I can't risk that. Here our own interests do come to the fore you see."

"So what do you propose now?" I asked.

"We give you the three days we're away to cool your heels. I think the best idea would be for you to be taken to our country headquarters again." De Laski seemed to be thinking aloud rather than addressing either Carlyle or us. "We can rely on everyone there. And I think you, Mr Minister Campbell," he said in a snide voice, "you'd better keep them company. I trust you to look after them well or it will be something you'll pay dearly for, that I can assure you. You may have forgotten in the heat of the moment, but we really can break you. That's why I can continue to trust you, you see. Now, we *do* have to go. The plane is waiting and it's a nine-hour flight even in the executive jet."

De Laski turned and started giving orders to Dobbs and to one of the American security men. I listened in fascination. It was a precise, clear and, to my mind, watertight list of instructions.

Four hours later and we were still waiting in Campbell's office. From the rushing around we gathered that the Bondi jet had developed some technical fault and it took much of that time to rectify it. The impatience and tension of the principal characters taught me a great deal about what had happened, and in the meantime we four were more or less ignored. We were forbidden to speak to each other, though, thankfully, we were brought coffee and a pile of foil-wrapped sandwiches for a late lunch. I asked for a whisky and was given a large one, undiluted and tepid. It helped me lapse into an easy limbo of detached disbelief. Perhaps for Ealasaid and Tesco it was more difficult than for the other two of us who had until so recently had all too much experience of enforced idleness. Once again, Guthrie sat grimly apart in one corner of the room.

The hours passed slowly. De Laski and Carlyle disappeared first, and then Dobbs left with Campbell. Dobbs obviously was also Dallas-bound. There were three armed guards now. They took it in turn to ferry us to the private lavatory off the adjoining room.

About quarter to six, Campbell returned alone. I sensed some new event. He appeared to have regained some self-confidence as he ordered one of the guards to telephone and let him know when the plane had taken off. Almost at once the message came back that they had left.

At the news Campbell took full control. He ordered the three guards to continue their security duties outside the room. They went reluctantly; it was contrary to their instructions. But they were mollified when Campbell explained that no one could possibly get out and escape if the guards remained stationed outside. He had important and delicate negotiations to conduct with us, I heard him whisper to the American guard commander. Mr de Laski wouldn't be pleased if they weren't to get anywhere in the negotiations because of the visible threat and presence of force.

As soon as they had gone, Campbell locked the door, turned and walked rapidly over to his desk. He opened the top drawer. "Have you noticed how remarkable it is," he said, "that the most fundamental things are ignored at moments of crisis and stress." He took out a gun, slammed the drawer shut again, and faced us. His other hand held a silencer; he clipped it on as he watched us. He must have practised.

"None of you are to move. I'll have no compunction about using it, and have every excuse if I do."

"What are you up to, Campbell?" I said shortly. "Stop the game-playing and let us out of here."

Campbell turned snarling and faced me. "You're all so blinkered," he said at once. "Especially you, Mockingham.

You assumed all along I was just a puppet dangling, waiting for others to pull the strings. But you're wrong, so wrong, Mockingham. Even Carlyle and de Laski didn't know how effectively I'd cut these strings a long time ago." I stared at him without comprehension.

In the far corner Tesco put up his hand, perhaps to sneeze, but he moved a fraction too quickly and Campbell spun round, gun all too ready. He was nervous, but had taken on the agility of a man deranged. Gone was the effete well-bred Campbell with his braying voice and drooping chin. Tension had contracted his facial muscles into a taut mask. "I said *don't move*," he hissed through clenched teeth. "And remember I don't mind who gets it first. You may think I'm a fool, but I can use this well enough." Tesco slowly dropped his hand to his side again.

Some time passed and I noticed Campbell glance up towards where a clock was fitted to the wall of the office. It showed two minutes to six. This seemed to have the effect of relaxing him slightly, for he sat himself casually on his desk, dangling his legs over the side as if he hadn't a care in the world. Only the pistol remained alertly poised in his right hand. For a good minute no one spoke.

"Come on, Campbell, give up before its too late; before you do someone an injury with that thing." MacDowall leant forward in his chair, quietly breaking the silence, like an old man advising a child. Campbell gave no sign of having heard, but sat swinging his legs, gazing from time to time at the clock on the wall.

"It's five minutes fast, d'you know that, Mockingham?" he said at last. "It has been for weeks, but this afternoon I checked specially to see that no one had put it right. I wanted to be sure you would understand."

"Be sure of what?" I asked. I was bemused by his manner, rapidly fluctuating as it did through the spectrum from hysteria to fey tranquillity.

"It's two minutes to six now, you see, even though the

clock shows three minutes past. So now it's about time."

We all sat staring at him. He had gone completely mad. He was smiling inanely to himself. Then he pulled himself together and became alert once again. He stood up and moved sideways towards the window, still facing us, the gun held tightly in his clenched hand.

"Mockingham. I've got a job for you. Come over to the desk and take the outside phone. I'm going to get you to ring someone for me and then you'll see who's been the fool, the puppet."

I stared at him uncomprehendingly.

"Come on now. Quickly. There isn't much time." He swung his pistol about violently. "I want to hear the last strings snap."

Obediently I wheeled myself over to the desk and picked up the receiver.

"You've got the dialing tone?—Good. Now ring the number you see written on the pad in front of you. When the Turnhouse Airport exchange answers, ask for the Control Tower. Give my name as authority and ask to speak to whoever's in charge."

I did as I was told and got through almost at once to the Chief Control Officer.

"Ask him if he's still in radio contact with the Special Flight that's just left with Carlyle and de Laski."

I passed on the question and, after a moment, the Officer replied smartly in the affirmative.

"Tell him to get on to the plane again now, while we wait. Tell the pilot there's a message for de Laski from me," said Campbell.

"What message?" I asked blankly. I didn't much relish this children's game.

"Just say that Campbell says goodbye."

"What?" I said incredulously.

"You heard. Go on or it will be too late." Campbell shouted. He banged the butt of the pistol down violently on the leather-topped desk.

Reluctantly I passed the message on. I heard the Chief Control Officer in the Control Tower hesitantly ask me to repeat the message. He asked whether I could confirm that such a mundane message was important. I didn't relish further argument with Campbell this end, so I said yes, yes it was. He could be told why later, I explained. I didn't know it, but I was right.

"Hold on till you hear the message has been passed," Campbell ordered me.

I obediently told the Officer that I would wait. I realised the man must have thought it was I who was mad. I looked at my watch. It was exactly six o'clock. The wall clock now showed five past.

The moment of truth dawned on me as I heard the puzzled voice of the Officer in the Control Tower explain that he had raised the plane and had been about to pass the message when contact was broken. It was too early to say, but the plane seemed to have disappeared from the radar screen as well.

I put the phone down slowly and stared hard at Campbell.

"Ah, so it's happened," Campbell said. "I can see it from your face. I hope de Laski got my message in time, I was looking forward to that bit. You know," he paused thoughtfully, "I was worried that Dobbs might decide to get someone to examine all the luggage. But he was a fool too. Yes, he was a fool too."

For perhaps five minutes we sat in silence, staring at Campbell while he swung his legs happily back and forward against the desk. He was humming gently to himself, but the slightest move and his gun came round expertly. Once someone came and knocked at the locked door of the room, and Campbell stirred himself sufficiently to shout that we were still in conference and weren't to be disturbed.

When at last he broke the silence he spoke clearly. His skin was stretched tightly over his face again.

"I have a second case, of course. This time I'm going to set it for six-thirty, or six thirty-five if you're going by the clock on the wall. Did you know I was in the Sappers once, Mockingham? I was quite good at my job now that I think of it. They even gave me an MC. Yet I'm not a brave man, Mockingham. Not now. After my Sergeant and that child were killed, they said I'd lost my nerve, that I'd run away. The court martial was a farce. I had an MC, and the good name of the Regiment was at stake, so they couldn't find me guilty. But it was true, Mockingham, I did run away. I ran because I wanted to live. It was them or me, and what was a French orphan and a dirty little Glaswegian sergeant to me?" As he spoke I noticed Campbell's eyes were red as if he had been crying. But there weren't any tears.

"Yes there's a case, and in the case there's a lot of explosive. You see it under my desk, Mockingham. A dark brown leather case, with my initials on it." He ignored everyone else and continued to address me alone. His few sentences told a great deal of story. There was a further silence.

Campbell turned slightly to glance out of the window at the rapidly darkening view, and Guthrie moved then. Launching himself from his chair, he hurled himself at Campbell and partially succeeded. But partially wasn't enough. There was a loud plop from the silenced gun and Guthrie lurched back and fell in a writhing heap on the floor. Ealasaid rushed forward and bent over the groaning body.

"Get back, you," Campbell shouted, fear flickering in his eyes. But Ealasaid, after glancing up briefly, ignored him and started to attend to Guthrie. I looked on with helpless horror as Campbell's finger began tightening on the trigger, but after what seemed an age, he relaxed, shrugged and in the schizophrenic way we had almost got accustomed to, appeared to forget about them.

"We must get him to a doctor," Ealasaid said. "He's bleeding badly."

Campbell stood up. "There's hardly time," he said as if to himself. "Five minutes isn't enough, you know." He smiled sweetly, but his eyes were vacant. I glanced at the clock. It showed six-thirty. Then the phone on the desk began to ring. Campbell picked up the receiver with his left hand. Someone was enquiring about the shot. "Champagne bottle exploding," Campbell said cheerfully and slammed down the receiver. There were now four minutes left, and I had no reason to doubt Campbell's timing.

"I tell you what I'm going to do," Campbell said. "In three minutes precisely I am going to leave this room after setting the charge, which I do by pulling a little wire you may see leading from the case to my desk. It's irreversible once it's set. I've calculated the amount of explosive very precisely and have added a bit to make sure. Once I've locked the door you will hardly be able to break out in one minute. Not least because you, Mockingham, and Guthrie here are hardly fit to assist. Then I will take refuge behind the plentiful supply of metal filing cabinets my generous Government have placed in the outer office. One can hardly wish for better armour plating against the blast. It will hardly be difficult to apportion blame for the explosions thereafter. You have demonstrably been plotting against the Government for some time, and poor de Laski and Carlyle too—you had a well-hatched plan which partially misfired, did you not?" Campbell stood up and reached over towards the thin thread of copper wire.

Something unplanned and uncontrolled welled up inside me. "Leave it, Campbell," I said, my voice as commanding as I have ever made it. He turned in amazement to look at me. Then he laughed.

I wheeled my chair across the floor into a position directly opposite him, and locked the wheels in preparation.

"You fool, Mockingham," Campbell said. "You poor crippled fool. And to think that I once was worried about you." He started to fumble for the copper wire.

"Give me that gun, Campbell," I repeated, "and leave your little bomb. Don't you realise you're finished? Too many people know, Campbell. You'll be hounded, Campbell." I saw his eyes flicker and a wisp of hesitation show as reality shone through for an instant. It gave me encouragement.

Then: "You poor wretched cripple," he said again.

"But you're wrong, Campbell," I said slowly. "You're mad or dreaming. I'm not crippled, Campbell. *You must be mad.*" I stared at him and caught his eyes. I dared not blink.

He started to laugh again. Then slowly, very slowly I stood up. He stared at me in amazement as I stretched out my hand towards him.

"Give me that gun, Campbell." I had hoped against hope that he didn't know. And he didn't.

"Give me that gun," I began to walk towards him, slowly but steadily, my hand stretched out to reach him and take the gun.

"*Give me that gun.*" He was breathing hard, eyes staring transfixed at the sight of my walking. But his gun was still pointing at my chest. I could almost reach him. Then sickeningly I knew that the shock of seeing me walk, my amateur attempt at hypnosis, was slipping rapidly away. It was too much and I had played it too late. He wasn't deranged enough to lower his defences for long.

But he had lowered them just long enough for Tesco to come round and hit him with a table lamp. He hit him very hard indeed.

TWENTY-TWO

THEY CAME AN hour ago and collected the battered cabin trunk. Now I am waiting, surrounded by suitcases, overcoat, briefcase and the shiny new pair of aluminium crutches. Ingram should be here at any moment.

I am alone, but I expect they will be at the VIP lounge to see me off. I am not looking forward to it.

The penultimate moment of departure is always a limbo if one is alone. But at this moment I can focus clearly, though the pain from my legs is there, as always, to bite at my mind. They will be there. Ealasaid will be there and will say goodbye. The others do not know it, but she will come and join me when her father's election campaign is over. Sir Alexander will be there; he has developed a political stature in keeping with his high reputation as manipulator of the Cabinet. I expect that in time he will fall heir to more than the late Prime Minister's constituency and seat in the National Assembly, since Matthews, solid though he is, cannot be but a temporary holder of the dead man's office.

They asked me to stay, to come back into the Government. But I told them I wanted to wait. Not all the Bondi slanders can be swept away overnight. So I accepted the Harvard offer of a visiting professorship in international relations. The duties are more honorary than onerous and I will have time to write up my material on John Law. I have arranged to get the Scottish papers airmailed to me, so I will be able to watch progress: the riots being contained; the slow progress of legislation in the Assembly and in the courts to nationalise the Bondi holdings. It will not be easy for Dr Mackinnon who is the Minister responsible, nor will it be for Matthews.

Many of them will be there. Tesco with his halitosis will be there. It is a pity; he is an able and likeable man, spoiled at the edges of his social behaviour. I cannot believe that he will settle here; he prefers American comforts. Guthrie will be there, on brief leave of absence from his convalescent home among the Cheviot Hills.

I have forgotten where they are holding Campbell. They expect him to live, though there may be extensive brain damage. Walt Tesco was upset about that, since he is by no means a violent man. He feels less guilty when he thinks, as we all do, about the fragments of de Laski and Carlyle and Dobbs scattered somewhere over the Firth of Clyde. And I have just remembered that MacManus, the man in Peterhead Jail who put me in my wheelchair, will today be going back to his wife and children, and at least I can feel charitable about that.

It will be a long struggle for me and for them. One battle in a long war, with no obvious winner. And why should I even mention Angela? Angela was my wife.

I reach over to the bottle of whisky on the hall stand, to pour myself a pre-journey drink, and knock over the glass. It is empty. It cracks but doesn't break. The bottle is almost empty too. I am sitting in an ordinary chair these days, lower than my wheelchair, and that could account for my clumsiness. I retrieve the cracked glass from under my chair and pour out a fair measure. It helps the pain, if not my nerves. I bend my head back, and shut my eyes for a moment, and see waves and waves and a child's sand-castle almost washed away. But the sand and the white pebbles and the shells remain.

From outside comes the sound of a car.

Sinclair
The dollar covenant